FADE OUT

BY LAURIE FAGEN

For Helen,
Thanks for your
support!! Enjoy

Laurie Fagen

Fade Out

A SHORT ON TIME BOOK:
Fast-paced and fun novels for readers on the go!

For more information, visit the website: www.shortontimebooks.com

The name "Find Me" is used with permission.

DEDICATION

For Geoffrey Dean Hancock
My dear husband of more than 25 years
who always encouraged my writing
and all my various, crazy activities.
Miss you so.

Also for my parents, Lowell and Lani Fagen,
who cheered me on in sports, music & writing,
and said I could be anything I wanted to be.
Thank you for still being positive role models.

ACKNOWLEDGEMENTS

My thanks to Publisher Karen Bryson at Short on Time Books for taking a chance on me, and to Ann Videan for introducing me to Karen through the ALWAYS writing group, a wonderful bunch of enthusiastic and supportive writers. As content editor, Ann was professional yet gentle in her constructive comments and guidance through the writing maze. Gratefully, my dear friend and eagle-eyed proofreader Sandy Vernon caught things that this normally fussy editor missed. My appreciation goes to cover designer and graphic artist extraordinaire Tad Smith for finding the perfect photo for this and future covers, and for a fabulous job creating the jacket design. Thanks also to first readers Linda Peters, Ann Videan, Deborah J Ledford, Susan Parker, Marla Hattabaugh, Pam Cannedy, Judy Rickard and Katherine Koenig for asking good story questions and giving great feedback.

Many thanks to a number of professionals who assisted in police and fire procedural areas, including Sherry Kiyler, former chief of police for Chandler Police Department; Dick McBlane, retired assistant chief for Chandler Fire Department; Phoenix Police Detective Timothy W. Moore; former Chicago Police Officer and Private Investigator Paul Huebl; and Chuck Fitzgerald, Battalion Chief Rural/Metro Fire and the crew of San Tan Valley Station 842. I take full responsibility for any other errors.

A cacophony of brash carnival sounds fills the air. Excited shrieks from people on midway rides pierce through engine noises, hawkers' taunts, and the music of a red, pink and blue carousel. Hot buttered popcorn and deep fat fried everything tantalizes fairgoers' noses.

"Step right up," a booming man's voice announces through a microphone. "Laay-dees and gentlemen, this way to the one, the only, the most amazing place you have ever seen!"

"Hey, let's check it out, Brad," a young woman says. "It looks like fun."

"Okay, Liz, but don't be mad at me if you get scared," Brad warns his girlfriend with a chuckle. "Two, please." Brad hands $10 to the man in the ticket booth.

"Thank you, sir," the carny says. "There's nothing to be afraid of in the Frightful Fun House." He laughs maniacally. "Unless you go in!"

Brad and Liz walk through the door and find themselves plunged into darkness. Somewhere, a woman screams.

CHAPTER 1

MONDAY, APRIL 8

" … with mostly sunny skies and an expected high of about 87 today. More news from KWLF News Radio right after this."

It's still dark outside KWLF-FM, a small radio station in Chandler, Arizona, and I'm the only one at work at the ridiculous hour of 4:45 a.m. Most 20-somethings I know would've been out partying last night and would be sleeping in or at least going to work at the normal time of 8 or 9. I'm sitting here in this tiny anchor booth, all by myself, these headsets smashing my long hair, talking into a mic, probably to no one. I mean, who is up listening to the radio except for insomniacs and maybe the few surviving farmers in this mostly urban area?

Time for a commercial. I touch a button and music starts, followed by a male announcer's voice hawking cars for a used auto lot.

I gingerly push an antiquated square audio cart into the machine. *One of these days we'll get real digital equipment.* Of course,

I think that every time I handle a piece of this older KWLF equipment, afraid it will crumble in my hand and we'll go off the air and...

Out of the corner of my eye, I see Grant Pope, our news director, enter from the back of the station. He takes off his hat and sticks it on a coatrack near the door. I wave, he waves back, but he looks tired as he heads to his desk. He's a short, thin man, with graying hair and a lot of lines on his face. These days his step isn't as springy as it used to be, and is he actually having trouble sitting down onto his chair?

He's been an institution here for more than 20 years, and one who has a "nose for news." I hear he came up through the ranks in the early days of radio as a reporter, anchor and then news director. He still writes frequent news stories, but several of my coworkers and I wonder when he's going to retire. He looks up, but I pretend I wasn't staring at him.

Another 30 seconds. I thumb through the news stories, change the order. The music and announcer's voice ends, and I turn my attention back to the microphone.

"This is KWLF news. I'm Lisa Powers, filling in for Pat Henderson. In this exclusive KWLF story, an East Valley woman says her father is missing, and she suspects foul play," I read from my script. "Joan Rogers-Hartley says her dad, 67-year-old Mark Rogers, took off early Sunday morning to drive to Northern Arizona for a bird watching trip—but never arrived. According to her, she thinks something is very wrong."

I tap a red button on the cart machine marked ROGERS-HARTLEY SOT, which starts Joan's voice.

"He was supposed to meet some friends of his in Clarkdale, where they were going to look for northern cardinals and red-winged hawks for a couple of days," Hartley says, sniffling. "But they said he never made it."

I continue. "Rogers-Hartley says Chandler police are quote 'dragging their feet,' unquote. KWLF Radio will follow this story and bring updates throughout the day. Anyone with any knowledge of the whereabouts of Mark Rogers is asked to call police.

"In other local news, the Chandler City Council meets in study session tonight to discuss rezoning of a large parcel of land initially slated for commercial development to be changed to residential. Grant Pope has details."

I hit a button and Grant's voice is heard. I lean back and listen.

Grant opens the door to the booth and pokes his head in.

"Was that missing man story on the wire?"

Uh-oh, I knew he'd ask that.

"Nope, the daughter called last night while I was here working on another story." I could tell by Grant's frown he wasn't pleased. "I know, I know, we don't usually do missing person stories until the police are called in, but that woman was really spooked. She seriously thinks he's in trouble. And we *did* get the exclusive..."

"All right, stay on it."

Yes! "Of course, I'll follow up as soon as Pat gets here. He *is* going to be in today, right?"

"As far as I—"

I hold up a finger to indicate silence, as the tagline "Grant Pope for KWLF Radio" is heard. As Grant slips out the door, I turn back to the mic and continue to read more news.

Spooky music plays over the sound of shuffling feet.

"Where are you? I can't see anything, Brad!" Liz says nervously.

"I'm right here, scaredy-cat," Brad responds. "Take my hand."

"I can't walk straight. What's up with this floor?"

"That's part of the Fun House, silly. They always have wacky floors that move up and down. Hey, see that red light? Head over that way."

There's a sudden high-powered blast of air.

"Eeeeeck!" Liz screams. "What was that?!"

"What was what?" Brad asks patronizingly.

"Oh, I guess it was just air shooting up. Jeez, how stupid...it just startled me."

"C'mon, let's see what else they've got here...if you can take it."

"Hey, I thought it was supposed to be a 'fun' house, too."

A door under the red light suddenly flies open with a "whoosh" and bright lights fill the room. Liz screams again, and bursts into laughter with Brad. As the floor undulates under their feet, they go through the open door.

"Oh, no!" Brad yells.

I'm glued to the three television monitors in the KWLF station, each tuned to a different local TV channel. Grant and Sally, the radio newsroom secretary, stroll over and watch as each carries the same woman's face and voice on their noon newscasts, standing in front of an upscale residential home in Chandler. Palm trees, lantana bushes, and other landscaping that manages to survive the Arizona heat ring the typical granite-rock front yard. No grass can be seen around the light-colored, two-story stucco house. Numerous microphones, like a metal floral bouquet, bloom in front of the woman's worried face as reporters and photographers gather around.

"He wouldn't just leave without saying something," the dark-haired woman says in a trembling voice, with tears streaking her face. Words superimposed on the screen read "Joan Rogers-Hartley, missing man's daughter." Joan turns her head toward an off-camera voice asking, "Was your dad having any financial troubles?" Her face clouds over with anger.

"Absolutely not! Why does everyone suspect *he's* done something wrong? He's a great dad. A gentle man who loves birds. This is just not like him. I'm afraid something is really wrong."

Joan turns to look straight into one of the cameras.

"But Dad, we're going to find you, don't worry!" She swivels her head back to the reporters. "That's all I have to say right now."

She turns sharply toward the house as the television cameras continue to follow her.

"So, you broke the story, Lisa," congratulates Sally, a co-worker in her 50s who already has mostly white hair. A little excess weight pulls the buttons taut on her pink blouse. "Way to go!" She high-fives me on her way back to her reception area desk. Sally is part cheerleader, part mother figure and prime schedule keeper for all those at KWLF.

"Okay, so I guess it was a good call," Grant says just a bit begrudgingly. "Keep on it."

I nod, holding back a bigger smile of satisfaction as I watch Grant head back to his desk. *I've got a nose for news, too,* I think just a little smugly.

I came to KWLF more by accident than on purpose, having responded to a "shadow day" offered by a local radio and television association during my broadcasting classes in college. I always assumed I would go into television news, but after spending the day at the radio station in my junior year at Arizona State University, I got an invitation from Grant to come back whenever I found time. I spent at least a couple of afternoons a week here, hanging around, listening, watching and asking questions of the other employees about the news business. I found I learned a lot by osmosis.

I was so excited when, in my senior year, Grant offered me a part-time job ripping wire copy, rewriting news releases, and going out with reporters on occasional stories. It eventually landed me a weekend on-air shift, and when I graduated, Grant hired me as a full-time reporter. I initially thought I'd only be at KWLF for a year or so, but now—three years later—I'm in no hurry to move on. I love going to the radio station every day, where each new story is an adrenaline rush.

A "ding" from my phone pulls me back. Time to head off to check my beat, which includes the courthouse, sheriff's office and police department.

"Hey, Joe, whatcha got working on the missing dad?"

With a small leather bag slung over my shoulder, holding a reporter's notepad and pen, I breeze through the door to the Chandler Police Department offices. There's still a faint smell of fresh paint from the recent remodeling effort at the downtown station that finally saw the older style metal desks that screamed "government" be replaced with more modern countertops, and included new carpeting. I glance at an old map on the wall marked "1960," when the city was only about 9,500 residents. The newer map next to it, labeled 2013, shows the population after a recent housing boom of almost 250,000. More citizens means more crime, and the department grew accordingly. I always thought the city was keeping pace fairly well, as I recall covering the opening of yet another new police substation in one of the latest suburbs.

My greeting is directed at Detective Joe Johnstone, one of the public information officers for the department, who is still furiously typing into his computer. Only in his early 40s, he's already balding, badly. He finally looks up when I reach his desk and slumps in his chair with an audible sigh, crumpling the cheap suit jacket tossed over the back.

"Why, I'm perfectly rotten, but thanks for asking anyway, and how are you?"

"Sorry," I say. "I'm fine. But you know how radio deadlines are..."

"Yeah, yeah, all work, no chit-chat," he says.

He's right, I'm not good at small talk. I subconsciously look down at my purple Crocs and signature khaki pants and nervously tug at the collar on my lavender polo shirt.

"We've put out a BOLO for his car, it's a..." he pauses while he searches for the details on his computer screen. "...a blue four-door 2006 Honda Civic," he reads. "His wife—"

I interrupt. "Sorry, may I record?"

I pull out a small digital device and microphone, press a button and hold the mic out. "Okay, a blue Honda Civic, 2006, four-door. You were saying about his wife?"

"Yeah, she saw him off around oh-three-hundred hours Sunday morning and went back to bed. His bird-watching friends he was supposed to meet around oh-seven-hundred just figured he was running late, so didn't try calling him 'til mid-morning. When they couldn't reach him by cell phone, they called his wife, a Janice Rogers, age 63, around noon. I guess you know about as much as we do after that. How'd you get the story?"

"I think it's because I was the only reporter the daughter was able to reach late on Sunday night. Any credit card or cell phone activity?"

Joe turns back to his computer and scans the screen. "Not that we've been able to find yet, but it's just been a little over 24 hours. Don't know how many missing person stories you've covered in your time, but thousands of adults disappear each year, and just being absent is not against the law. Adults can take off if they want to, and they don't always tell their families."

"I understand that, but his daughter, Joan, says..."

"Yes, I know what she says. Told me every which way what a great guy her dad is, how this is out of the ordinary for him, yada yada yada. Do you know how many times I've heard that?"

"But, if he was your—" I start.

"Hey, if he was my dad, I'd figure he's probably drunker'n a skunk in some joint up on Whiskey Row, and he'll come back with his tail between his legs in a day or two."

I pause, blinking a couple of times. I can't imagine thinking of my father that way. Richard Powers is a well-respected businessman in central Iowa, working in the insurance industry for more than 30 years. My parents' idea of drinking was serving a bottle of Mogen David wine every year for their anniversary. "She seemed pretty convinced that he's not like..." I begin, but realize by the middle of the sentence most people in that position would be the same way. I change my tack. "So, what's the next step?"

"Give him a few more hours to get his act together. In the meantime, we'll start doing some preliminary investigating."

"Thanks, Joe. Anything else you working?"

"That—and the usual barking dogs, domestics and thefts because people forget to close their damned garage doors—are gonna keep us pretty busy for a while." He turns his attention back to his computer as I put my recorder and mic back in the bag and start to leave. But I stop and turn back around.

"Got any cold cases?" I ask expectantly.

"I was hoping you'd ask." Johnstone looks up with a grin, reaching for a manila folder in a drawer. "Here. See what you can do with this one." He tosses it on an empty desk. "You know the drill."

"Thanks, Joe." *All right!* A surge of excitement courses through me. I put my bag down and take a seat at the table.

Number four cold case for Chandler PD, I count as I glance over the cover page. Last winter, my friend Ron, a former radio reporter, and I found the killer of a young woman about my age, discovered strangled to death in 1992.

For me, the easy part is simply reading through the police files and officers' notes, but it's time the stretched department can't dedicate to an officer. With the many advances in forensic science, I basically suggest new tests to run on the evidence. I can't quite explain the gut instincts or hunches that tend to pop into my head. Sometimes I dismiss them, but most of the time they turn out to be pretty accurate.

I open the file and read. The case, dated June 1985, is about businessman Dwayne Meyers, age 43, a White male, president and CEO of a small community bank, who disappeared for several days before being found shot dead in an abandoned warehouse.

It was in the middle of the savings-and-loan debacle of the '80s, and as a local banker, Meyers was over-lending to developers with few assets who were buying land and starting questionable commercial and residential projects. His bank was one of many in trouble, and police initially thought Meyers took off because he was overextended and wanted to avoid his mounting debts.

Even when a ransom call was received after a couple of days, police were still skeptical, suspecting Meyers of faking the kidnapping to get money. His bank put up the sum requested and dropped it off at a specified location. The money was taken, but something happened and police missed the pickup.

Then a call came in with a location as to where to find Meyers, but when police arrived, he was dead, tied to a chair, his hands, ankles and mouth bound with duct tape. He had been killed at point-blank range with two shots to the head and one in the heart. No one ever found a trace of the killer or killers.

I spread out the black and white photos on the desk. One, a smiling corporate headshot of a handsome Meyers; another portrait of Meyers with a pretty woman, presumably his wife, and two small children. There are several more gory pictures from the warehouse: Meyers slumped in a chair, a pool of blood at his feet; close-ups of the tape around his wrists and ankles, attached to a metal folding chair. Mesmerized by the images, I stare at them, trying to remember every detail.

I pick up the warehouse picture of the dead Meyers and study it. *Bare feet? Expensive shoes nearby. Pricy suit, too. Did he want to make a good impression or was he doing better than people thought? His wife received a $5 million life insurance payoff following his death. A lot of money,* I think.

I take out my notepad, and scribble: *check ballistics and run bullets through registry again.* I consider the newer technology available today and write: *Reexamine duct tape for prints and DNA that could link to killers; ck with forensic linguistics about ransom call; talk to widow, see how she and children are doing.* I do some quick math to see Mrs. Meyers would be 64 now, the son and daughter 32 and 34.

It's another clear and sunny spring day as I walk the two blocks from PD back to the radio station. Usually I think about how diffferent it is from the cold and snow in my Iowa hometown. Normally I smirk a bit, thinking about my friends and family there, suffering through blizzards and bundling up in heavy jackets, boots, gloves and scarves. But today, my mind is not on the weather, nor on the traffic rushing by as I talk on my cell phone through a wireless earpiece.

"...oh, and just like you said, Johnstone is totally trying to disregard the foul play possibility from that missing dad case," I say.

I know Ron Thompson, age 68 and a former "cop shop" radio reporter, lives vicariously through me. Known back in the day for his gruff reporting style, Ron practically resided at the Phoenix Police Department during his career. He would start his mornings at 5:30 a.m., as did many who woke up listening to him on KTGH Radio, announcing the overnight reports of crime in his gravelly, no-nonsense way. He took me under his wing the year before he retired, and has taught me a lot in the short time I've known him.

"Yeah, figured he would," Ron replies. "Stay on him."

"I will," I answer. "You game for a possible field trip?" I worry about his health, but I know he relishes being involved in the crime stories I cover.

"I thought you'd never ask," Ron chuckles.

"Oh, and do you remember what was referred to as the 'savings-and-loan debacle' of the '80s?"

"Remember it? Ha—I lived it! Yep, Charlie Keating and his band of merry senators," Ron laughs, which turns into a deep cough. Ron's COPD lung disease often makes it hard for him to breathe.

"Ron, you okay? You got your O_2 on?"

"Yeah, yeah," Ron says, a little short of breath. "I gotta go. Recording session still on for tomorrow?"

"Only if you're up to it," I say tentatively. "We can resched—"

"No way, bring your stuff and we'll do it."

"Okay, Ron, see ya soon." I tap off my phone with a smile. I'm at the back door of the radio station, ready to enter, when a large calico cat comes from behind the dumpster.

"Hi, pretty momma, how are you today?"

The feral cat, obviously very pregnant, looks at me with suspicion, but inches forward cautiously. I dig in my pocket and bring out a small plastic bag of cat food.

"Here, sweet thing, you need this for those babies of yours," I coo, as I empty the sack on the ground. "Tomorrow I'll bring a bowl."

I remember my idyllic days growing up on a farm in rural Iowa. *Well, idyllic now perhaps,* I muse. *Sure didn't like those harsh winters, early morning chores and never having much money for extras.*

My family always had cats around, but the "mousers" usually stayed near the barn, doing their job to keep the vermin population down. We had a housedog, but never housecats, except for the short time when a baby kitty was practically mauled by one of the outdoor dogs, and my youngest brother brought it into the house. Amazingly, our indoor dog, Nipper, who had raised many litters of pups, took care of the kitten, even producing milk for it. Poor cat never really knew what kind of an animal it was after that. I've always wanted a kitty, but with my schedule, I don't think I could take care of one properly.

I watch for a moment as the hungry feline devours the meal, and head inside.

It's mid-afternoon as I check email in my space at the newsroom's bullpen table, yawning from being up so early. The KWLF sports anchor, Dan, is in the booth, his voice booming over the speakers, animatedly debating who would be the winner of the NCAA men's championship tournament. It was coming down to the Final Four after a series of upsets in the popular games.

Police scanners squawk with dispatcher calls and officer voices, while the AP Radio News feed drones on in the background.

Grant sees me looking tired, and walks over.

"Got anything else for today?" he asks.

I lean back in the chair. "Not really. PD is taking their time with the missing dad, but they did find another cold case for me." My eyebrows rise, showing my enthusiasm.

Grant smiles. "You've had a long day. Why don't you kick off?"

I am beat, but I hesitate to let on. "No, really, I'm fine."

"You may be, but I have to watch everyone's overtime. See you at your normal time tomorrow morning."

"Oh. Okay, Grant. See you then." I gather up my belongings and head out to the parking lot. I'm not usually off this early in the afternoon, and I know my refrigerator is pretty bare. I make a mental note to make a trip to the grocery store.

Once outside, I don't see the mother cat, but the food I brought earlier is gone. *That's a good sign,* I smile, as I go to my car. I run my finger along the smooth, cherry red paint on the second hand Dodge, thinking of my dad who bought it after my college graduation. I have driven it back and forth across the country a couple of times already, as well as to California, and the vehicle has served me well.

As soon as I climb inside, my cell phone rings. The caller ID says Bruce Erickson, the weekend sports anchor at a local TV station who seems to have some romantic interest in me. I'm a little hesitant to become too involved again, having recently broken up with a lawyer in the district attorney's office. As I told Nathanial "Nate" Rickford, I have aspirations other than a small radio station in Chandler. I'm not planning to stay here forever, and I know a career move or two or five might be in store for me. That's the norm for broadcast journalists, but Nate has a child from a first marriage, and was not interested in moving around. *Bruce is certainly persistent,* I think.

"Hey, Bruce, what's up?"

"Geez, Lisa, what's a guy gotta do to talk to you? Don't you ever answer your voicemail?" I can tell he's teasing—mostly. I punch the speakerphone on and start my car.

"Sorry, I'm on the phone so much with work. Email is the best way to get me." I look up the street and pull my car into traffic.

"Oh, that's exciting. So I'm s'posed to use email to ask you out?"

Yikes...stall. "You want to go out?"

"Yeah, why is that such a shock? I thought we had a good time in the Suns' skybox a few weeks ago."

"That was fun." I recall having a fairly enjoyable evening, glad for the number of people around. Not like a real date. "I've just been...pretty busy."

"Yeah, well, that's life in the media, and it means you're working. Not busy, well, then you're 'between opportunities.' Not a great place to be."

"Good point." I pause. *Do I really want to encourage this?*

"So, you wanna have dinner Friday night?" Bruce asks.

"I'm not sure how my Friday's gonna go yet. You working this weekend?"

"Yep, and every Saturday and Sunday." I sense disappointment in his voice.

"How about a rain check for early next week? There's a new restaurant opening in downtown Chandler. Maybe we can try it out."

"Okay, but I'm going to hold you to it."

I know you will. "Thanks, Bruce. Talk to you later."

"Bye."

My smile fades as I end the call and continue to drive home.

Mysterious music fades up full and under, and my voice begins.

"Welcome back to 'Murder in the Air Mystery Theatre.' I'm Lauren Price. Tonight on 'Frightful Fun House: Brad and Liz are having a blast in the carnival fun house. Or are they? When we left them

last, they just entered another room…and Brad is shocked at what he
sees."

Spooky music fades in and out from all sides of the room, and there
are sound effects of the shuffling of feet.

"Oh, no!" Brad yells.

"What?!" Liz screams behind him.

"Look…you…you're huge!" Brad sees Liz's reflection in a room full
of mirrors, and she has been transformed into a short, very obese
woman. He laughs uproariously. Liz is not so amused.

"Very funny, Brad," she says coldly, as she moves to another mirror.
This one makes her look nine feet tall and skinny as a blade of grass.
"Hey, just give me a volleyball and I'll spike one right on your head,"
she adds.

Meanwhile, Brad moves to another mirror that contorts his body
into a continuous "Z" shape. "What do you think, Liz? Am I coming
or going?" he chuckles.

As the couple makes their way around to the various mirrors, each
reflecting a different contortion of their bodies, a door opens from
nowhere. A clown, complete with red wig, painted face and huge
shoes, runs in, screaming in terror and carrying an axe high above his
head. He heads right toward a shrieking Liz before continuing
through yet another mirror-turned-door-turned-mirror. Brad grabs
Liz's hand, chasing after the colorful character.

"Let's see where that clown goes!"

But when they try to open the mirror-door, it is solid and unmov-
ing.

"I don't know about this anymore, Brad," Liz whines. "Let's get
outta here."

"Well, we would...if we could." Brad looks around. "Any idea where the exit is?"

They feel along every mirror, but find no doors, no signs and no way to leave.

Suddenly, the lights go out.

"Braaaaaad!" Liz screams. But Brad never answers.

"Will Brad and Liz get out of the Frightful Fun House in one piece? Stay tuned for the next podcast of 'Murder in the Air Mystery Theatre.' I'm Lauren Price...thanks for listening."

From my home computer, I enter a few keystrokes. The screen shows the podcast is saved, and I finish the last sip from my glass of white wine and turn off the monitor.

CHAPTER 2

TUESDAY, APRIL 9

I park in the KWLF lot and pull my gear bag over a shoulder. To-day I've brought two small plastic bowls, one filled with crunchy cat food, and I set it not far from the back door.

"Hey, pretty momma, where are you?" I call, looking around for the pregnant calico. Not seeing her, I walk in the back door to KWLF. Grant's at his desk, talking on the phone, a cup of coffee in his hand. I give him a wave, and he acknowledges me with an upward motion from his dark eyebrows.

Just stepping inside this newsroom each day makes my stomach flutter with exhilaration. There's always something exciting about not knowing what stories I will get to work on. Sure, it's a small station with minimal staff, but I feel like an integral part of it.

Anchor Pat Henderson's rich, deep voice booms out from the speaker. I always think he sounds like the actor, James Earl Jones, and rather looks like him, too.

"It's 7:45 a.m. on KWLF Radio. In the news, Chandler police are still looking into the mysterious disappearance of an area man," Henderson says. "Lisa Powers has this story."

My recorded voice filters around the newsroom. I stop to listen.

"It's now been about 48 hours since 67-year-old Mark Rogers left for a bird watching trip in Northern Arizona, but never arrived. Chandler Police say there has been no cell phone activity, and no one has heard or seen him since he left his home early Sunday morning. His family—daughter Joan Rogers-Hartley is the spokesperson—is adamant that he wouldn't just take off, and they fear something is very wrong."

"He's always been a good father, a loving husband," says Rogers-Hartley on tape. "He wouldn't just leave without saying something."

I fill up the second plastic bowl with water from the drinking fountain, and walk to the back door, still listening to my story.

My voice is heard again. "Rogers-Hartley says she knows of no financial problems her parents were dealing with, saying they've always been generous with gifts. Rogers-Hartley adds that she and her father last talked around two o'clock Saturday, and discussed his upcoming trip and a funny noise in her car. She says he agreed to look at the vehicle when he was back on Monday. According to her, he sounded just fine."

"Like normal," says Rogers-Hartley. "Like any other day. There was absolutely no indication that he was upset about anything, or that anything was out of the ordinary."

My voice continues.

"She says she believes they have lost valuable time because police would not take the case seriously. Police say being missing is not a crime. KWLF will continue to follow this story. Lisa Powers, KWLF News."

Need to call Joan and see if anything's new today. I take the bowl of water outside and put it next to the cat food, but still see no sign of the mother cat. I head back in, sit down at my desk and power up my computer. Pat's voice comes back on, but I manage to tune him out as I check email. I scroll through a number of news releases from various PR people, nonprofit organizations and listeners wanting the station to cover or run a story on their causes.

I see a message from Detective Johnstone, sent at 6:40 a.m., and I open it.

Lisa,

The evidence boxes on the Meyers cold case are in my office. Sgt. Hoffman is working it and can meet with you tomorrow at 0900.

Joe

Great! I get a surge of adrenaline as I check my online calendar. I'm adding the item for tomorrow when I hear a slow series of tones—first low and then louder—come over the fire department scanner in the newsroom. I look up at Grant, and we both hurry to turn up the volume.

A female computer-aided dispatch voice sounds.

"Three and one structure fire, engine 281, engine 282, ladder 281, battalion 281, rescue 281, 4-2-8 South Ashley Street, report of house fire with explosions..."

"House fire, go!" Grant shouts to me, as I instinctively grab my bag with recorder and mic. "I'll call David to get the live van and meet you there. Don't forget pictures for the web." He's scribbling down the address as the dispatch voice comes on again.

"Multiple callers state large house. Unknown if occupants are inside."

I race out the back door and jump in my car. As I start it up, I try to talk calmly into my phone: "4-2-8 South Ashley Street." I pop in my earpiece and drive out of the parking lot onto the still relatively quiet street.

My cell's GPS begins giving directions. "In 500 feet, turn left onto Arizona Avenue."

I drive with my knee as I check my recorder in the bag. I plug in the mic and run a quick test. "Testing one, two, three." The red needle bounces. I put both hands back on the wheel and look up to see a huge cloud of black smoke in the distance.

"Oh, man," I say out loud. My heart is racing. Dark smoke like that generally indicates a fire burning out of control, with no water pumping from fire trucks yet.

An older-model vehicle, driving very slowly, dawdles in front of me. "Move, move!" I hear a siren and see flashing lights in my rearview mirror. I pull my car over to the right of the road, and the other car follows suit. My cell phone rings, with the caller ID saying KWLF. I tap my earpiece.

"Jeez, huge plume of smoke. Still black. I'm about five minutes away," I say. "Got a ladder truck racing down Arizona Ave. I'll be right behind them."

I recall covering another smaller house fire last year with one of the KWLF reporters, but I was really just observing. This one is definitely already much bigger, and I know I am on my own this time to cover it. I shake off the nervous flutters in my stomach.

"They're calling for more units," Grant explains. "It's a large house in the Circle G subdivision. Fully engulfed. Still not sure if anyone is inside."

While stopped, I take digital photos and a video of the billowing smoke, blackening the otherwise blue sky. *I'll post these to the website later.* The red-and-white Chandler fire truck passes me, and I'm able to whip my car back on the road, ahead of the other slower driver.

"Okay, thanks. Did you get David?"

"Yeah, he's on his way. Coming from Gilbert."

"10-4, thanks."

I keep the fire truck in my sight as it turns.

My GPS gives an update. "In half a mile, turn left onto Chandler Heights Road."

I make the same turn, and realize both my hands are clutching the steering wheel too tightly. I loosen my grip and take a deep breath. *Chill. You can do this.*

The GPS interrupts my pep talk. "Turn right onto Riggs Ranch Road."

The fire truck already made the bend. The black cloud of smoke curls into the air, higher and higher. Its dark swirls are mesmerizing. I almost get lost in the nearly hypnotic patterns they create.

"Ahead, turn right onto South Ashley Street. Then your destination is on the left."

I punch off the GPS and follow a truck marked "Battalion" as it stops on the side of the street. I race out, throwing my bag over my shoulder as I run toward Battalion Chief Andy Hernandez. The muscled Latino, a familiar sight on fire scenes, climbs out of his department vehicle. We both stop to look at the two-story upscale McMansion, as huge orange flames dance out of every window and plumes of thick, dark smoke pour angrily upwards. Just ahead of them, a solo fire truck finally sprays some water on the fire, but it's a small stream in comparison. Other trucks continue to set up and begin attempting to fight the fire.

"Chief!" I shout. "What do you know so far?"

He turns toward me. "Not much yet. Neighbors reported seeing smoke, then heard something explode. The fire spread rapidly."

"Anyone inside?"

"We don't know," the chief says. "A woman named Rosemary Thornton lives there, but we haven't been able to get close enough yet, let alone inside."

Thornton, Thornton, how do I know that name? "Is that the Thornton of the pharmaceutical family?" I ask.

"Not sure, might be," he answers. "Gotta go." He heads back to the vehicle.

More fire trucks respond, and a TV news truck from the NBC affiliate races in. Just behind it is the KWLF live van, with a determined looking David Brooks at the wheel. I get his attention and wave him over, and he pulls the vehicle in as I snap a few more shots of the blaze and upload them to the KWLF website's home page. Out of the corner of my eye, I see Bruce Erickson jump out of the TV truck and start to set up equipment with his videographer.

With the radio station's satellite dish up and the battalion chief standing by for an interview, I get ready to do my initial report. I note Bruce and his crew are still adjusting their TV equipment, and I get a little thrill knowing I will be the first to go live. I listen to my earpiece, waiting for the cue. The station's "breaking news" music begins, and Pat Henderson intros the story.

"A first-alarm fire in Southern Chandler is still raging at this hour. Our Lisa Powers is on the scene and has this report."

"Thanks, Pat," I say into my mic, still watching the blaze and the frantic efforts of fire fighters. "At least six Chandler fire trucks are attempting to put out a huge house fire at 428 South Ashley, in the upscale Circle G Ranch development. Gilbert fire trucks are on their way as are responders from Rural Metro Fire Department. Battalion Chief Andy Hernandez says neighbors heard an explosion, then saw smoke. Chief, any idea yet what started this inferno?" I turn to the spokesman and point the mic toward his mouth.

"Not at this time," Hernandez says. "If there was an explosion, it's possible it was due to natural gas. We've shut down the gas lines, but we won't know until we get the fire out and start our investigation."

"We understand this home belonged to Rosemary Thornton, heir to the Thornton Pharmaceutical Company," I ask. "Was there anyone in the house?"

"We have not found anyone yet, but it's been a defensive fire up to now. We were just able to safely get a couple of our firefighters in the house with a thermal imaging camera, and they are still looking."

"Thank you, Chief," I say as the man turns back to his staging area. "Again, fire caused by a possible natural gas explosion at a Southern Chandler home is still burning at this time, and…"

A deafening crash rumbles the air, and for some reason, I instinctively duck as I turn to see the location of the sound. *Crap, what was that?!* Shouts from first responders intensify as firefighters quickly retreat away from the blaze, and two, completely covered in fire gear, run outside to safety.

"Lisa? What's going on? You're still on the air." Grant's voice is in her ear.

Get it together! I try to gather my composure as I face the blaze again. "Oh my goodness, the…it looks like…I think the second story roof fell in. As Battalion Chief Andy Hernandez just told us, they had firefighters inside looking for any survivors, and we just saw two firemen escape from the house. Again, the roof of what is believed to be the two-story mansion of Rosemary Thornton has apparently collapsed as this fire rages on. Fire officials have not yet determined if anyone is inside. We'll have more as this story develops. I'm Lisa Powers, reporting live for KWLF Radio. Back to you, Pat."

Pat Henderson continues with the news. I hand my mic back to David, and notice my hand is shaking. "Wow, I guess that was good timing," I say with a weak chuckle as I snap a few more still shots. I grab my recorder and head back to the fire scene. "I'm going to try to see if I can talk to a neighbor."

"10-4," David replies. "We're back on in 17 minutes."

I take a deep breath and head out across the street. *Did I stutter very much during that last report? Jeez, I can hardly remember what I said.* I sure hope, in all the excitement, it made sense and was accurate.

I spot a small crowd of local residents watching the fire, and head over, prepping my gear. They huddle around each other, some still in robes, others with jackets thrown on to ward off the morning chill.

"Hi, I'm Lisa Powers with KWLF radio," I say. "Did any of you hear an explosion?"

"Yeah, I did," said one man in his 40s.

I begin to record his voice. "Can you tell us what you heard and saw?"

"Well, it was almost 8 o'clock, and I was getting ready to leave for work, when I hear this big 'boom.' It even rattled some of my windows. So, I look outside and here's this huge fire. I called 9-1-1, but someone else had already reported it."

"Do you know Rosemary Thornton who lives there?"

"Nah, I don't really know her," the man says. "I see her Mercedes coming and going, but I rarely see her."

"Anybody else familiar with her?"

"I knew her father," an older woman interjects. "But she stays pretty much to herself."

"How about her husband? Anyone seen him?"

The residents look at each other with slight smirks on their faces.

"What?" I ask. *That's a curious reaction to what I thought was a basic question.*

"Well, it's her third, and he's about 20 years younger than she is," one says with a shake of his head. "His truck is gone. Prob'ly went *fishing*." He emphasizes the word facetiously and sneers. "He does that a lot."

"Oh." I make a note on my pad. "So, have any of you seen Rosemary this morning?"

The group looks at each other, puzzled expressions on their faces.

"Uh, no, we haven't," one says. "Do you think...?" He doesn't finish the awful question.

"Fire says they haven't found anyone inside," I add quickly.

The group shares a moment of relief.

"Thanks, may I get your names?" I ask, and gather some additional information. My gut tells me there may not be a good outcome for the owner of the house.

By late morning, the firefighters begin to get an upper hand, and the once thick, black smoke has turned white with the dousing of water to the fire. The majority of flames are under control, but the house is a literal shell of its former self. The roof and most of its supports have collapsed, and smoke still pours out of the blown out lower-floor windows. Black, charred trees and bushes surround the house, and grimy water runs down the driveway to the curb. Gray ash floats lazily in the air like fluffy, dirty snowflakes. I take more photos and upload them to the station.

All three local television news stations now have their live trucks on the scene, with satellite dishes boosted to the top of tall poles. Reporters, including Bruce, do stand-ups in front of cameras to cover the breaking news story. Two TV helicopters drone in a circle overhead, getting aerial shots.

Suddenly, a firefighter runs out of the burning structure, shouting instructions. I can't quite make it out, so I hurry toward the battalion chief's truck. I also hear squawks on fire department walkie-talkies that signal an obvious change in the scene, and a Chandler Fire Department paramedic engine backs into a closer position. Two firefighter paramedics climb out, open the back doors and pull out a gurney. As I'm getting both still and video shots on my camera, I notice they are not in any big hurry to move into the house. My stomach lurches.

"David! Something's happening. Get us live!"

David gives a thumbs-up in response. I use my phone as a walkie-talkie.

"KWLF, do you copy? Can you send it out to us?" *Hurry, hurry!* I wait for a reply.

"Lisa, this is Grant, what's up?"

"I think they may have found someone inside. Paramedics are going in." My insides are doing flip flops as I watch the scene.

"How soon can you go live?" Grant asks.

David gives another thumbs-up signal.

"We're ready as soon as you are," I say. *Settle down. You've got this. Big breath.*

"Okay, stand by, in about 15 seconds," Grant answers.

I take a big gulp of smoky air. Holding my hand against the earpiece to hear the station's cue, I make sure to keep an eye on the house. I flip my camera over to David and point at the house, to indicate that he should take photos. David signals I am live.

"Yes, Pat, we may have a new development at the house fire in Circle G Ranch," I report, still watching the burning building. "Chandler fire paramedics are now taking a gurney into what's left of the Rosemary Thornton mansion here in the 400 block of South Ashley Street.

"The first-alarm fire saw about 15 various Chandler units responding, including others from Gilbert Fire and Rural Metro, to what neighbors describe as a huge explosion and incredibly large flames that quickly engulfed the structure. It is considered under control at this hour, with mostly smoke and only a few small fires remaining in the charred remains of the home. However, emergency medical personnel do not seem to be in a hurry going into what's left of this house, which leads us to believe that they have found someone inside. Someone who may not be able to be rescued.

"Residents report that pharmaceutical heiress Rosemary Thornton was living in the house, but no one could recall seeing her this morning. Repeating, the huge house fire at 428 South Ashley in Southern Chandler is now under control, and fire paramedics are inside with a gurney to retrieve what is possibly...wait, here they come, pushing the gurney back out..."

Damn, this doesn't look good. I point a finger at David to get the still shots and I continue.

"It looks like...yes, there is a black body bag on top of the gurney with something inside, but it is zipped up, indicating possibly a dead body from the fire, although this is not yet confirmed. Deaths by fire typically require dental records for identification, as often the bodies are burned beyond recognition. If that is the case, we will continue to cover this story and bring you the latest in what may now be a residential fire with a possible fatality. Reporting live, I'm Lisa Powers for KWLF Radio."

Grim faces of paramedics and firefighters gather around the gurney as it continues down the sidewalk to the waiting emergency unit. I get the camera back from David and snap more photos as I see one firefighter make eye contact with Battalion Chief Hernandez and shake his head somberly. Hernandez nods in affirmation and says something into his walkie-talkie.

I run over toward Hernandez, and Bruce and other reporters and photographers quickly gather around as well. I begin recording, but I already know what he's about to say. I've covered fatalities before, but it still sickens me, knowing it's someone's daughter, wife, friend, who is now dead.

It's early evening in the newsroom at KWLF, and David and I debrief the "night crew"—consisting of one on-air anchor/reporter

—about the events of the fire. A large computer monitor with the station's website shows our photos of the scene.

Grant holds his coat and hat in hand, ready to head out. Station Manager Terry Tompkins, a tall, lean man wearing an expensive suit and carrying a briefcase, walks into the newsroom, and sniffs.

"Did the copy machine finally catch on fire?" he quips.

"Sorry, Mr. Tompkins, David and I reek from the house fire we—"

"Oh, I know, I know," Tompkins interrupts. "Well done out there, young lady. Great photos. And all that dental record stuff. Impressive."

"Oh, hey, too much watching Forensic Files, I guess." I know my face is blushing.

"Good work, but go home and take a shower. Orders!" Tompkins heads out toward the back door.

"Yes, sir," I smile. My heart warms with pride at the compliments.

Grant puts on his hat and starts to follow Tompkins.

"I second that motion," he says. "Good job. See you tomorrow." He pauses. "Oh…uh, take your time coming in if you want. Keep your overtime down."

The heat and steam fill my small bathroom, clouding over the mirror. In addition to washing away the smells and grime of the day, the hot water kneads my tired and sore shoulder and back muscles. It helps relieve the stress of five live shots, seven interviews and two additional news stories I cut back at the station. Not to mention posting a couple dozen fire photos and videos to the KWLF website.

I let the pounding water pour over me for just a few more minutes. I had to cancel the podcast recording session with Ron because of all the day's activities, but he understood, and told me how proud he was of my good reporting. I smile when I recall his claim that I was "almost" as good as he was at my age.

Realizing I need to upload my latest edited podcast, I turn off the water and reach for the towel.

The murder mystery podcast theme music fades in, and my voice begins.

Welcome back once again to 'Murder in the Air Mystery Theatre.' I'm Lauren Price.

After walking over an undulating section of floor and into a distortion mirror room, Brad and Liz are plunged into darkness.

"Brad? Where are you? Answer me, damn it!" Liz waves her arms around in the darkness, trying to find him, a way out, anything. But she's met only with silence.

"Brad, this isn't funny! I want outta here, now!"

Suddenly a low, ominous rumbling begins somewhere in front of Liz. The entire floor begins to tremble, and gaining momentum, shakes more and more. Liz can't hold on to anything, she can't see anything around her and she falls to the floor.

"What's going on?" she cries. "Brad!"

Liz hears a "whoosh" sound, like a huge wind, and suddenly she's sliding, down, around, down farther into the pitch-blackness.

"Noooooo!" she shrieks.

Where is Liz heading? And where is Brad? What's next in the Frightful Fun House for our carnival couple? Stay tuned when the next podcast of 'Murder in the Air Mystery Theatre' continues. I'm Lauren Price...thanks for listening.

CHAPTER 3

WEDNESDAY, APRIL 10

At 8 in the morning, I would normally be at the station, ready to work. But with Grant's admonition about OT, I enjoy another cup of coffee while leisurely reading the newspaper comics on my iPad, a treat usually left for last thing in the day. While I typically never sit around much, yesterday took a bit of a toll, and I was enjoying the relaxed morning for a change. I gather the remains of a daily and two local community newspapers that clutter my small kitchen table and pitch them in the recycling basket.

Sounds from a morning TV news show drone on from a small portable set sitting next to a larger flat screen in the nearby living room. With the picture-in-picture turned on, all three images show different stations. My ears perk up when I hear "fire fatality" from one of them. I grab a remote and turn up the volume.

"Chandler Police confirm that a badly burned body was found in the rubble of one of the city's largest fires in recent memory," anchorwoman Jennifer Rhodes, a young brunette, reads into the camera from the set.

Yep, had that last night. The picture changes to footage of the blaze at its height as the anchor continues her voiceover.

"The 57-hundred-square-foot home went up in flames following an explosion, fire officials say, and when firefighters were able to get inside, they found the body in what's believed to be the living room. While there's no positive ID yet, police expect it may be the owner, 62-year-old Rosemary Thornton, heir to the Thornton Pharmaceutical Company and daughter of its founder, Jeffrey Thornton."

A still photo of Rosemary fills the screen with a logo of Thornton Pharmaceutical. The photo changes to that of a handsome young man.

"According to neighbors, Rosemary Thornton's third husband, Tyler Jameson, was possibly out fishing on his boat in Saguaro Lake at the time of the fire. However, authorities say they have not been able to contact him yet, nor has he returned repeated phone calls from KTTK."

Hmmm, handsome guy, and much younger than Rosemary.

The camera comes back to Rhodes.

"Police say dental records are being sent to the medical examiner's office. Cause of the fire has not yet been determined."

Had that, too. I know I shouldn't feel quite so arrogant, but it's always good to beat the competition, especially a big TV station.

The anchor pauses for a beat. "Now, let's take a look at today's weather with Dimitri Contos."

I'd normally turn the sound back down, but I want to see what, if any, particular weather is in store for Northern Arizona later this week, in case Ron and I can go looking for Joan's dad. The weatherman's report is no big surprise for late spring in the Sonoran Desert: mid to upper 70s, sunny skies with little wind and no precipitation expected. *Just another rotten day in paradise.*

My normal nervous energy back, I pick up my cell phone and speed dial Detective Johnstone.

"Hey, Joe," I say when he answers. "Will the medical examiner autopsy Rosemary Thornton's body from the house fire?"

"Oh, yeah. Body was already taken to the M.E.'s office yesterday. It's required by law any time there's a death from violence of almost any type—gunshot wounds, stab wounds, blunt trauma—and it includes fire deaths. Pretty standard."

"How long for the report?"

"Usually six to eight weeks."

"Really? That long?"

"Again, standard. Haven't heard anything out of the ordinary on this one, so, once the autopsy is done, and the death certificate is signed, the family can dispose of the remains."

I let that sink in for a moment. "Okay, thanks much, bye." After ending the call, I wait a second, and dial the station.

"Hey, Grant, it's Lisa. I see that—" I start to say, but he interrupts.

"I'm fine, sir, feeling great, thanks. And you?" Not one for small talk, I go through the motions with my boss.

"Yes, I heard that same report, and I thought I could start pulling info about Rosemary, the charities she raised money for.

You know, a little about her life since everyone seems to believe it's probably her."

I listen for a moment. "Okay, sure. Oh, a reminder, I have an appointment on that savings-and-loan cold case with Sgt. Hoffman this morning at 9, so I'll be in around 10."

I say goodbye, and click off the phone. *Hope that evidence box has the dead man's clothes and shoes,* as I make a mental note. I finish reading the newspaper cartoons.

As I drive to PD with the radio station on in my car, I can imagine Pat Henderson sitting in the KWLF control room, headsets on, reading the top of the 9 o'clock morning news. He begins with the latest story I left the night before.

"New information on that Chandler man who left for a trip to Northern Arizona but never arrived. Lisa Powers has this report:"

"A development in the case of the missing Chandler man who was to go bird watching south of Flagstaff near Clarkdale with friends, but never showed up and hasn't been heard from all week. Police say a debit card receipt shows 67-year-old Mark Rogers stopped at a convenience store at Cordes Junction Sunday morning and bought a soda and chips. No activity has been shown on his card since. His family, especially daughter Joan Rogers-Hartley, feel understandably distraught at his disappearance."

"We are asking for anyone who might have seen him, talked to him…anything…to please call us or call police," his daughter pleads. "He is a responsible man, a great father, and we just know something bad has happened. He would never leave without calling us."

My voice continues.

"Rogers is a retired Intel engineer, married for 48 years and, according to his daughter, not having any marital or financial problems. He was driving a blue 2006 Honda Civic four-door on his way to a bird watching trip with three buddies north of Clarkdale, but never connected with them. Police continue to investigate. Lisa Powers, KWLF news."

"It's 9:03 and 75 degrees at KWLF News. More news after this." Pat punches a button and music from a commercial begins.

A variety of papers and photos cover the oval wooden table in the Chandler PD conference room, and evidence boxes rim its perimeter in neat stacks. Sgt. Edward Hoffman, in his mid-50s and wearing a dark suit, looks up from reading a file when I knock at the door.

"Hi, I'm Lisa Powers from KWLF Radio."

"Ah, yes, recognize your voice. C'mon in," he gestures.

I put my equipment bag on a chair and walk around the table. *Yes! Like discovering buried treasure.* My excitement mounts as I view the old case boxes, but I try to remain professional. "Looks like you've got a lot more information about this case than the first one I worked on. You know, the Native American moccasin maker who killed his girlfriend about 18 years ago?"

"Right. Good work on that one, although we all caught a little grief from higher ups about you and your radio buddy going out on that interview without backup." Sgt. Hoffman raises an eyebrow in my direction.

Oh jeez, not that again. "I know, I know. But we really didn't have any firm evidence, and I didn't want you guys wasting your time."

"Hey, we appreciate your help with these old cases, but you gotta follow some protocol, especially since you're a civilian." Hoffman closes his file.

"Roger that, Sergeant," I salute, and he cracks a smile. "So, I have a few questions about some of the old evidence." I pull out a skinny spiral notebook from my bag.

"Shoot," Hoffman says.

"Back in 1985, were police able to lift any fingerprints from the duct tape wrapped about the victim's legs?"

"Hmmm, let's see." Hoffman walks around the table and selects a manila file. "Looks like maybe one partial, but not enough to ID anyone."

"Well, in the Casey Anthony trial, forensics experts used a reflective ultraviolet imaging system to highlight existing fingerprints on a piece of duct tape. And I read about a trial in Texas where a crime scene investigator lifted prints from duct tape from a 25-year-old case—by freezing the tape and pulling the layers apart."

"Now, how on earth would you know all that, young lady?"

"Uh, I read a lot. And I have a friend—who used to be a photographer for Channel 6—who now owns a forensics company to study video and audio. He is an amazing resource."

"Okay, then. Guess that's worth checking out." Hoffman made notes on a yellow legal pad. "What else?"

"Of course, DNA testing not available at the time might reveal something on the tape about the killers," I offer.

"That's pretty standard, but I'll check on it."

"What calibre of weapon was used?" I ask.

Hoffman looks through the notes. "Looks like it was a .38 revolver. Unfortunately, there are literally millions in existence."

"I'm sure the bullets found in and around the victim were run through ballistics at the time—would it be worth sending them through again? Maybe the murder weapon was hidden for some time but might've reappeared."

"You've really done your homework. What's your angle on all this?"

Same thing Mom asks all the time. "Oh, ya know, combination of a mystery needing to be solved, along with a little morbid sense of curiosity, I suppose."

"If we weren't short-staffed and didn't have so many other crazy suspects to chase around, we might get more of these cold cases solved, or at least looked at again. Anything else?"

"Just one more thing: do you know where the victim's wife is now? Any idea how she and her kids are doing after getting that $5 million dollar life insurance money?"

"Good question." Hoffman picks up another file. He opens it and thumbs through the papers inside. "Looks like she moved outta state the year he died, went to Southern California...um, Rancho Palos Verdes? Ever hear of it?"

"Oh, yeah," I reply. "A good friend of mine got married there." *Should I tell him how ritzy Rancho PV is? How the cheapest homes there start at $3 mil and go up?*

Hoffman flips another page. "Says here she also remarried about a year later, then divorced and moved to Sedona."

Yes, another field trip, I think to myself. "I believe she was 28 at the time, so she'd be about 64 now. Her two kids would be young adults now."

"I'm sure we can track her down," Hoffman says, closing the file.

"Great, let me know. I'd love to be in on the ballistics testing, if possible?" I raise my eyebrows with hope.

"Let me see what I can do. I have no idea how soon forensics can take a look. But give me your phone number and I'll keep you posted."

I hand him a business card. "Thanks, Sergeant. I'll follow-up in a couple weeks. Meanwhile, may I look through some of the physical evidence?"

"Okay, but remember: Anything in bags, don't—"

I interrupt. "I know, don't open, don't touch, don't remove. Got it. Any photocopies need to go through Joe."

"Let me know if you find anything interesting," the sergeant says as he leaves the room.

Best part of the job, I think as I walk around the table, lifting up the cardboard lids of evidence boxes, looking for something other than paper files.

When peeking under the lid of the fourth box, I find the crime scene items I'm looking for. I carefully pull out a large paper bag marked DWAYNE MEYERS JACKET. It has a clear plastic window running the length of the bag, and I can see Meyers' dark gray suit coat. It looks like it's folded to show a hole in the back with a dark, dry stain that runs down the jacket, thick at the top, and thinner toward the bottom. There's also a dark stain around the collar, presumably from the two gunshots to the head. *Shot in the back. What cowards.*

I try to find the label, but it's not visible through the little window. I lay it on the table, and write in my notebook: *Ck maker of Meyers' suit.*

Another bag holds a lighter silvery gray, subtly striped men's shirt, this time folded to show the left front of the shirt. The section contains a significantly greater amount of blood around another obvious bullet hole.

A third bag holds a pair of black shoes—GUCCI, according to the marking inside—and a fourth holds a beautiful lavender silk tie, but I can't see any particular stains on them.

Also in the cardboard box is a long and skinny plastic bag containing strips of traditional silver duct tape, marked "victim wrists." I look further and find a similar one marked "victim ankles." *Do today's criminals ever get caught using purple or zebra-striped duct tapes on the market today?* I can see a few small droplets of a dark brown color on the wrist tape. *Spatter from the gunshots?* I can't see any blood on the tape used to bind Meyers' ankles, but I lay them aside and make another note: *Ck for prints on ankle and wrist tape.*

A large paper bag with the same plastic window holds Meyers' suit pants and socks together. It looks like the fibers had been pulled from the pant legs when the duct tape was removed, but I don't see any fuzzy strings pulled in the same way from the socks.

I put the evidence bags back, and open a thick file. Black-and-white photos of the crime scene spill out. One shows Meyers from the back, slumped in a chair, his hands bound and blood streaking down the back of his suit jacket. I look closely at the wide shot from the front revealing the dead man fully dressed—except with bare feet.

Hmmm. Gotta be something about having his shoes and socks off.

I make another note. I thumb through the other photos, read from case files, and make additional notes. *Get DNA sample from wife, others from bank to rule out.* I go through the lab reports, but don't see anything about fibers. I make another note: *Ck fibers for hair, other.* I type into my Droid calendar: *Send Q to Sgt. Hoffman.*

My digital watch beeps. I glance at the time, 10 a.m., and I put the files and other evidence back in the boxes. I quickly gather my belongings, take a satisfying look at the room and head out.

Another beautiful day in the Arizona desert. I walk the short distance to KWLF, the sun warm on my face. Fumes from cars rushing by on a packed Arizona Avenue attack my nostrils. *Who decided that this stretch, which is also a state highway, would go through the small historic city center?* The 1912 square is now a bustling destination on the weekends, and once in a while, friends and I check out the busy restaurants and bars. But I also know some of the soccer moms from the higher-end housing developments just five minutes south are nervous about venturing into the area with the Hispanic barrio only a couple of blocks away.

I call Ron on my cell.

"So, all the TV stations love 'reporter involvement,' right?" I say into my wireless earpiece as I turn the corner to the station. "Why not radio?"

"That's the point," Ron replies. "You can do a radio interview over the phone, you don't have to do it in person with cameras like on TV. But you gotta get this past Pope."

"Yeah, I know." *That may be a tough one. What will make him say yes?* "Talking face-to-face with the cold case vic's ex-wife in Sedona might give us new information." I pause, thinking. "I s'pose with the early shift and long day with the fire, I could do it on my own over the weekend—"

"No way," Ron interrupts. "They need to pay you for your time. Is this the field trip you were talking about?"

"One of possibly two. So, could you go? Up and back on Friday? I know Grant would feel better knowing I wasn't by myself."

"Let me see how I feel tomorrow, and I'll let you know."

"Sounds good."

The chirping of a text message on her phone interrupts. "Hey, gotta go. Talk to you later."

I punch a couple of buttons to see Bruce's message on my screen: *bunch of us getting 2gether at irish pub at 7. join us?*

I look at the calendar on my phone. *sorry, got a recording session 2nite. another time.* I add "thx" and press Send.

Arriving at the station, I look again for the pregnant cat. Both bowls by the door are empty, so I fill up one with food and pour water from my bottle in the other.

"Here kitty, kitty," I call, but to no avail.

A group of Boy Scouts tours the newsroom as I arrive. I drop my bag onto a rolling chair, take a big breath and head over to Grant's desk.

"Grant, I'd like to speak with—" I begin.

"Oh, Lisa," Grant interrupts. "Got a message from a neighbor of Rosemary Thornton's. They said to call right away. Sounds urgent."

He hands her a pink message slip.

"Uh, thanks, I'll give 'em a call." *Darn, I'll have to wait to talk to him about the road trip later.* I go back to my desk and dial the number.

"Hi, this is Lisa from KWLF, I had a message to—" I stop abruptly and listen. "Thanks so much, I'll be right there!"

I grab my bags. "Chandler Fire investigators are at the mansion. I'm heading over to see what they find," I say over my shoulder.

"Don't forget web photos," he yells after me. I wave in acknowledgment and head out the door.

I count five fire personnel wearing masks working at the Thornton home. Two take photographs, another places items inside plastic bags, a couple more sift through the ashes, one with a rake. An older man and woman sit on the porch next door, watching.

Walking around the yellow fire scene tape gently flapping in the light breeze, I remember the intense fire and smoke of just a day ago, and my heart picks up its tempo at the thought. Today there's mostly wet, gray soot and muddy residue, with a few tiny smoke curls rising from the center of the once opulent house. Structural beams have toppled. Yellow-gray insulation flops out from the exposed walls. The skeletal remains of burnt furniture sit in place as if waiting for their mistress to return. *So sad to see this beautiful home destroyed. It must've been quite the showcase.* I take a few digital photos with my camera.

I spot Battalion Chief Hernandez in his vehicle, talking on his cell phone. I walk over, making sure he sees me, and wait for him to finish his call.

When his window rolls down, I walk closer, smiling.

"Good morning, Chief. What have you found so far?"

Hernandez picks up his hard hat from the seat and opens the door. He puts the helmet on his head and adjusts the neck strap.

"We're just getting started," he says, and walks toward the remains of the home.

"May I watch for a while? I won't get in the way," I ask.

"Just stay outside the tape and you won't."

I watch as Hernandez approaches one of the investigators, a burly man who takes off his hard hat, revealing a short military-type haircut. The man rubs his head as if in frustration as he talks to the chief. I take a shot of the men.

I walk slowly around the tape, getting as close as I can, peering into the debris, snapping photos. *Hmmm, the majority of the damage seems to be on the east side of the house.* Going around the corner, I look through the green bushes to see a large melted TV screen still attached to what's left of the south wall. I continue around, taking more photos and noting in my reporter's pad that the bushes in the front and back of the mansion are charred black.

From the rear of the home, I look through a huge hole and spot a bright bit of color. *What's that? A lamp? Oh, one of those antique stained glass types from the 1920s.* I get a shot of it as it lies on the floor, surrounded by muck and burned furniture. It catches the light from the sun above, as if a reminder of better days.

I stop. *What's that smell? Something sweet? Amid all this charred wood?* I sniff again, not finding the odor, but write a note. *Hmmm, and it's gone. Weird.* I resume my stroll, continuing to photograph around the north side of the home, where the walls are still mostly in place and there's less fire damage.

Rounding the corner back to the front of the ruins, I see Hernandez once again on his mobile, standing near where the front door used to be. I walk past him, looking again at the very charred remains of the bushes on the east side.

"Can you tell me why the landscaping here and on the west side is so much more badly damaged than those on the south side?" I ask Hernandez when he pockets his phone. He takes a look at where I'm pointing and heads my way.

"It's possible that was a primary location of the fire, but it's too soon to…"

"What's that smell?" I interrupt. "Something sweet, kinda flowery." I sniff again.

Hernandez inhales a couple of times. "Hmmm," he says with a frown, walking closer to the house. "Rincon!" he says, motioning to the military-haircut guy, who walks cautiously toward him. The two move their heads closer together and talk in low tones. Rincon flips through a small notebook, shaking his head. Hernandez points toward the center of the mostly damaged area, and Rincon carefully walks back in.

"Stop by HQ later," Hernandez shouts toward me. "Maybe we'll have something by end of the day."

I smile and head back to my vehicle, snapping one last wide shot of the scene.

Back at my desk, I search through websites of nonprofit organizations that Rosemary Thornton was involved in. There are photos of smiling women dressed in gorgeous ball gowns, blinged out in diamonds, with Rosemary in the center of most of them. A short platinum blonde woman, a little overweight, pops up in many of the pictures, but usually on the far edge, like she slipped into the photo at the last minute. I make a note of one Janet Fradley, and when I Google her, I find Janet is in many of the same organizations as Rosemary. I find a phone number, but just as I start to pick up the handset, it rings. Startled, I jump, pulling my hand back as if it was burned. *Sheesh! Chill already.* I answer the phone as my heart settles down.

"Lisa Powers, KWLF Radio."

"Lisa, you won't believe this great organization we found!" Joan Rogers-Hartley says, her voice filled with excitement. "It's called 'Find Me' and they help search for missing people. They use dogs...and psychics."

"Psychics? Really? Are they legit?" *That might make an interesting story.* I grab a pad of paper and start taking notes.

"Oh, yes, in fact the group is made up of a bunch of retired law enforcement personnel, founded by a former DEA agent. And they think Dad is still alive!"

"Well, that's great. What do they base it on?"

"One of the psychics was given the case—they don't charge a penny either—and she believes he's alive, but hurt."

"Wow, that's amazing. Are you still going to retrace his steps?"

"Yes, we're heading up the freeway first thing Friday morning."

"I may be going to Sedona on another story Friday with a friend. How about if we join you?"

"Well, I don't know. We don't want a bunch of cameras..."

"Um, I'm a radio reporter. No cameras. Just a couple extra pairs of eyes and ears to help look for your dad."

"Oh, right. Well, okay, we'll be heading out of the Valley around 7."

"How about if we meet you at the Cordes Junction exit where your dad stopped for a snack, around 8?"

"Sounds good, thanks."

I hang up, make a note in my cell phone calendar, and pick up the phone again to try Janet Fradley. On the other end, it rings and rings, and I am about to hang up when I hear a slurred "H'lo?"

"Hi, I'm calling about the Cultural Commission," I say. "Is this Janet Fradley?"

"Uh, yeah, right, thish ish Janet," the female voice replies. *Wow, is she drunk or high?* Loud music pounds in the background.

"Well, I wondered if I could ask you a few questions about the organization. Um, just where are you, if I may ask?"

"Oh, I'm over here havin' a few drinksh with my friendsh at O'Toole's. Why doncha come on down and I'll tell ya all about those old fuddy-duddies!" Janet laughs uproariously.

I look at my watch. *It's only 1:30 in the afternoon.*

"Okay, I'll be there in a few minutes," shaking my head as I hang up.

As I gather my things, Grant comes by my desk. "Did you want to see me about something earlier?"

"Oh, um, it can wait. I've got to meet a woman who I think knows Rosemary Thornton. I'll be back in a little bit."

O'Toole's is an Irish pub in the historic downtown square, with thousands of dollar bills stapled to the walls and ceiling. The lunch crowd is thinning, but a number of drinkers laugh it up at the bar. I recognize Janet from the photos and approach her.

"Hi, Janet, I'm..."

"Well, yer jus' in time to have a Snakebite with us," Janet interrupts, raising her glass of cider and Guinness. "Barkeep, get thish young lady a drink!"

Janet's hair is wild and unkempt, and the ends of her bangs are frizzy halfway up her forehead. Her red-rimmed brown eyes are barely half open. Her blouse shows too much cleavage, and her short skirt is hiked up high as she struggles to stay perched on a stool. One high-heeled shoe lies on its side on the floor.

"Maybe this isn't a good time," I start, but Janet grabs me by the arm.

"'Course ish a good time!" Janet squeals, plunking me down next to her.

"So, I saw some photos of you and Rosemary Thornton," I say. "Did you know..."

"Rosemary?" Janet's face falls. She tries to focus on me as tears well up in her eyes. "Oh, poor, poor Rosie," Janet slurs. "She was such a...well, I mean, ol' Rosemary thought she was so...Ya know, everybody loved Rosie, or at least they loved her money..." Janet takes a gulp of her drink, spilling some down her blouse.

"Oh, now look wha' I did." Janet clumsily tries to mop up the spill. "Rosie would never do anything so shtupid. But she sure made me feel shtupid sometimes..." Janet's voice trailed off.

"How did she do that?" I ask.

"Rosemary always got the besht positions...the besht dresses...the besht guys," Janet mumbles, her head thumping down on the bar. "But no more, nosirree..."

"What are you—" I start, but the bartender interrupts.

"Okay, lady, we're cutting you off," the bartender says, taking away her drink. "You a friend of hers? I think she's had enough."

I agree to take Janet to her house. I get Janet's shoe on, place the drunk woman's purse over a shoulder, and help her out to the car.

"Janet, I'm taking you home," I say firmly as I pour her into the front seat. "Where do you live?"

Janet's head rolls from side to side as she continues to speak unintelligibly about "never good enough." I open Janet's purse to retrieve her wallet. I find her driver's license, punch the address into my phone's GPS, and start to put the wallet back. I spot a baggie of white powder with a red skull and crossbones printed on it. *What the hell is that?* I slip the plastic sack out of Janet's purse and into my recording bag.

Janet looks as if she's falling asleep as I pull out of the parking space and head down the street. But when the male voice on my phone gives directions, Janet wakes up with a frightened look on her face.

"Ty, baby, ishat you?" She looks wildly around, and grabs the steering wheel.

"No, Janet, stop!" I scream, turning the car just before we hit a parked vehicle.

"I gotta talk to Ty!" Janet yells, once again trying to grab at my hands, and redirecting my Dodge into the path of an oncoming auto. The other driver maneuvers away at the last second, blasting the horn. I pull off to the side of the street and turn off the car.

"Janet! I have to get you home! You've had way too much to drink."

"Ty, he lovesh me, not her," Janet mumbles.

"Who is Ty?" I ask, but Janet is close to falling asleep again.

"Ty hashn't called me, he won't ansher his phone, oh Ty baby..." she moans.

I shake my head. "Maybe you'd like to stretch out in the back seat?"

"Um, hmmm," Janet murmurs, attempting to open the car door. I jump out and help her into the back, where she curls up and closes her eyes.

I gently close the door to Janet's bedroom, after making sure the woman is fast asleep. I tiptoe quietly around the small apartment, peering into drawers.

In the kitchen, I sniff. *There's that sweet smell again.* I walk around, trying to find the source. I open a cabinet door under the kitchen sink, and inhale a second time. Pulling out a small trash-can, there's a pair of blue latex gloves on top that are torn, as if taken off in haste. I find a plastic baggie in a kitchen drawer, and envelope the gloves, closing the top.

I open Janet's purse, pulling out the woman's cell phone. I scroll through the "recent" calls and one name appears time after time after time: Tyler Jameson, Rosemary Thornton's husband. I make a note of his cell number.

I let myself out silently.

I drive a little too fast, back through town.

"Ron, you won't believe what I found!" I say in a jumble of words. "Look, I can't tell you everything right now, 'cause I have to get down to the fire department before five, and I still have to talk to Grant."

I turn a corner, tires squealing. "Do you know any independent drug testing labs in town?" I race through an intersection where the light has already turned yellow. "Great, would you call them and see what their turnaround time is? Then I'll tell you all about it at our recording session tonight."

I wheel into a Chandler city lot, turn into a parking spot and slam on my brakes. I turn off the engine and sit for a moment, eyes closed, collecting my thoughts and willing my heartbeat to slow down. When my breathing eases, I gingerly pull out the small sack of white powder I found in Janet's purse. I hesitate and study the unknown substance. Making sure no one is watching me, I wrap it in a tissue and put it into the glove compartment. I get out and make doubly certain my car doors are locked.

I like walking through the lobby of the Chandler Fire Department, with its modern silver metal outlines, trimmed in bright fire engine red paint.

The faces of firefighters who lost their lives in the line of duty hang on one wall, and their eyes seem to follow me as I walk through. Against another wall sits a rusted piece of metal, enshrined in glass, a section of steel beam from the ruins of the 9/11

World Trade Center terrorist attacks in New York City. I pause for a moment in front of it. *I was 13. What a horrible day that was.*

"May I help you?" a voice through a speaker interrupts my thoughts.

I turn around and spot a video monitor up high framing the face of a woman in her 40s.

"Oh, yes, I'm Lisa Powers, here to see Lieutenant Rincon."

"Through the door, to your left, Room 182," the woman says, and a buzzer indicates the unlocking of the door.

I find Rincon behind an older government-issue desk, his Marine-style haircut uncovered. He makes a note in a manila file folder, and shuts it as I approach.

"Hi, Lieutenant, I'm Lisa Powers—"

"From the radio station," he interrupts, standing. He puts out his hand, which I take, feeling a little too firm of a handshake. "You here about the Thornton fire, too?"

"Yes, I'm sure you've been inundated, but Chief Hernandez said—"

He cuts me off again.

"No additional information as of yet," he says brusquely. "We are still working the case." He sits back down. *Trying to stonewall me? I can play that game, too.*

"So, was there enough of the body left to autopsy?"

"Talk to the M.E."

"Did her husband have any explanation as to the cause of the fire?"

"We have nothing to release on that at this—"

"What kind of accelerant was found?" I interrupt Rincon this time, who looks up with a glare.

"How do you know about that?" he asks suspiciously.

"Well, the explosions heard by neighbors, the massive fire, all points to arson, right?"

"We have not determined arson nor will we discuss anything further until—"

"But do you deny that something must have helped spread the fire?"

"No...I mean, yes, I mean, I have no further comment!" Rincon's face flushes.

"Thanks, I'll be touch," I smile as I exit his office, leaving him staring angrily at me.

I pace back and forth outside the back of the KWLF station's employee entrance, hardly noticing a slim-bellied calico cat.

It's a perfect situation for getting a reporter really involved, I think to myself. *And I'm hopefully getting two stories out of only one trip, and besides Ron Thompson will be with me, or at least I hope so.*

Just as I reach for the handle, the heavy blue security door opens toward me, and Grant walks out, hat on his head, carrying his briefcase.

"Oh, 'scuse me," I say. "Grant, I wanted to—"

"Sorry, I have a meeting at the university in a few minutes. Can it wait 'til tomorrow?"

I smile. *Foiled again.* "Sure, no problem. Have a nice evening."

I watch for a moment as he heads to his car, and let out a big sigh. I'm about to go inside when I see the momma cat, significantly leaner.

"Hey, pretty momma, how are...oh my gosh, did you have your babies?" I start to rush forward toward the cat, but it spooks and runs away. "I'm sorry, kitty, didn't mean to scare you." I pause, looking around. "Where are those little ones of yours?"

It's after 8 in the evening, and the kitchen table in Ron's house serves as an Internet production studio, with my laptop computer, microphones and various items to be used for sound effects.

Ron sits at the table, turning the packet of white powder over in his large hands.

"...and she was so drunk, she almost made me run into another car," I recall.

"But how did you find this stuff?"

"She was so out of it, she couldn't even tell me where she lived. So I looked in her purse to get an address from her driver's license, and that's when I spotted it. Any idea what it might be?"

"If it was illegal crack or meth, it probably wouldn't have the warning symbol on it."

"Here's enough in another little baggie for your friend to test." I hand it to Ron and take the larger amount from him. "I need to get this back in Janet's purse without her knowing."

"And just how are you going to do that, young lady?" Ron looks at me over his reading glasses.

"Well, I haven't figured it out yet," I say with a weak smile. "Oh, I almost forgot," I add, digging into my bag and pulling out the plastic sack with the blue latex gloves. "Would you ask your buddy to see if he can tell what's on these?"

"And where did you get those, Miss Junior Detective?" Ron frowns as he takes the item.

"Found 'em in the trash, no big deal."

"Yeah, right." Ron puts the baggie in his pocket. "I'll see what I can do."

I pick up a script. "So, you ready to start?"

"Don't change the subject," Ron warns. "You have to be cautious. That broad sounds like a wacko."

"I know, I know, I'll be careful. Promise. Ready?"

"Whenever you are," Ron says. He pulls off his pale green oxygen tubes, typically feeding into his nose, until they hang loosely around his neck. He adjusts headsets over his ears. A mic on a table stand sits in front of him, and he picks up the script.

"Mics on, here we go," I say, tapping a few keys on my computer keyboard.

The haunting theme song for "Murder in the Air Mystery Theatre" begins. I lean into the microphone and read from my script.

"*Good evening, I'm Lauren Price. Tonight on 'Murder in the Air Mystery Theatre,' we continue the story of the carnival couple thrust into a Frightful Fun House. Liz can't find Brad, and she's just tumbled down a long slide.*"

I pick up and drop a large telephone book on the table with a "thud." I continue reading from the script: *Liz stops suddenly as the slide ends, and realizes she's lying on what feels like plastic balls. It's still dark, and she can't see a thing.*

I cue Ron, who shuffles a bag of plastic balls near his mic, and I read again. *She feels all around her, rolling every which way on the balls, before touching what she thinks is a person.*

"*Brad?*" I whisper as Liz. "*Is that you?*"

"*Ohhhh, wha...*" Ron, in his Brad voice, groans. "*Liz? Liz? Where are you?*"

"*Oh my god, Brad, thank god it's you! Are you okay? What happened?*"

"*It...I...don't have a clue. One second we're in that mirror room, and the next it's like the floor has gone out from under me, and I fall down a long chute or something. I think I passed out for a few minutes...then I heard you. Are you okay?*"

"*Yes, but this is not fun anymore. We've got to find a way out. Hang on, I've got a flashlight app on my cell phone.*"

I make shuffling noises.

"*There, that's bet—oh my god, Brad!*" I read. *Liz holds the light up to see Brad with a nasty bump on his forehead, and a little blood dripping from his nose.* "*We've got to call police, or somebody!*" *She tries punching 9-1-1.* "*Damn, no cell service.*"

She moves the light around the room. "*Okay, see if you find a door,*" I read.

They're surrounded by thousands of blue, green, red and yellow plastic balls. A sign that reads "Insanitorium" begins to glow from across the room—above what looks like an exit.

"*There!*" Brad points. "*That's got to be a way out!*"

The mysterious theme music fades in, followed by my voice.

"Will Brad and Liz find an exit from the Frightful Fun House? Be listening next time when 'Murder in the Air Mystery Theatre' continues. Thanks for listening...this is Lauren Price."

"That was a great one," I say, chuckling. "I gotta tell you: I really appreciate you doing these podcast shows with me."

Ron pulls his headphones down around his neck. "Hey, it's something different. I can tell you still like cranking out these stories, don't you?"

"After writing hard news all day, it's a good creative outlet. And writing fiction means I can just make stuff up, which is fun. Are you up to doing another?"

"Bring it on," Ron says eagerly.

CHAPTER 4

THURSDAY, APRIL 11

I make my morning beat check run to the police department and sheriff's office, but don't find much in the way of news stories. Back at the station, there's nothing much in the way of emails either. I take a sip of coffee, look through a file folder and find a number. I pick up the phone and dial.

"Maricopa County Medical Examiner, Sherrell speaking."

"Hi, this is Lisa Powers from KWLF Radio. May I speak to Dr. Douglas?"

"Sorry, he's not available. Can I take a message?" Sherrell sounds harried.

"When is a good time to call?"

"Uh, looks like he's doing autopsies all day. I'll give him a message and he might be able to call you back in between."

"Can you confirm that he is doing an autopsy on Rosemary Thornton? She died in that big house fire Tuesday."

"Let me see. Yeah, looks like it's on the schedule for later today."

"Great, thanks. Please have Dr. Douglas call me when he can." I leave my contact info and hang up.

I pick up my coffee cup and head to the kitchen. The newsroom secretary, Sally, is heating up something in the microwave. She manages to keep everyone in the newsroom organized and where they're supposed to be. She likes "mothering" us, and enjoys finding out the news before her friends.

"Hey, Sally, have you seen that wild calico cat out back?" I pour a cup of decaf and add cream and Stevia from a packet.

"Oh, once in a while. She's pretty skittish." Sally pulls out an egg and sausage meal.

"She was very pregnant, but I think she might've had her kittens. If you see or hear them, let me know?"

"*You* want to take care of baby kitties?" Sally asks a bit incredulously.

"Gosh no, not me. I just want to make sure they're okay."

Sally sits down at a kitchen table, opens up a newspaper and reads while she eats. I head back to my desk, pick up the phone again and dial.

"Hello, is this Denise Meyers?" I ask when the connection goes through.

There's a long pause. "Who's calling, please?"

"My name is Lisa Powers, and I'm a reporter for KWLF radio in Chandler, looking into your husband's cold—"

"He was my ex-husband," the woman interrupts. "My name is Richardson now."

"Oh, I see, thanks for that. Like I said, I am looking into his death as part of the cold case files for Chandler Police, and I wondered if—"

"Why on earth are you calling me? Has there been some new development? How come the police didn't contact me directly? If I find out—"

"Wait a minute, Mrs. Richardson, no, there's nothing new on the case. But that's why I'm looking into it—to find new information, perhaps test old evidence with new technology, and see if we can bring his killers to justice."

"Ha," she laughs snidely. "Like that could ever happen." There's another long pause.

"Actually, there have been some fantastic enhancements in fingerprint technology that I think might—"

"What do you want from me?" Denise interjects sharply.

"I'd just like to speak with you about Dwayne, his work, and what's happened since he was killed. A lot of times with these older—"

"What do you mean, what's happened since? Nothing has happened, there's nothing to talk about. I don't know anything." Denise's voice is curt.

Hmmm, quite defensive. "As I was saying, in some of these cases, the perpetrators might have confided in someone about it, and years later people are willing to talk. Could we come visit you Friday in Sedona? We just need about an hour."

"I don't know, I think it's a huge waste of your time."

"Wouldn't you like to have some closure regarding Dwayne's death? Don't you want it to be over, once and for all?"

There's another pause. "That's all I've ever hoped for," Denise says quietly. I hear a long sigh.

"All right. Here's my address."

I add the information to the file. I turn back to my computer and write:

ANNOUNCER VOICEOVER:

In our continuing "Cold Case Conundrum" series from the Chandler Police Department, this week KWLF investigates the murder of a businessman during the savings-and-loan debacle of the 1980s, found shot to death without a trace of the killers. Reporter Lisa Powers has more details in an attempt to help police solve this case:

LISA VOICEOVER:

Arizona was a hot spot of imprudent real estate lending during the 1980s and '90s, leading to a widespread savings-and-loan crisis. That's when hundreds of financial institutions here and across the country failed—and many high-ranking political figures of the day found their careers cut short when implicated in an influence-peddling scheme. It was an embarrassing time—but it rarely led to death.

Except in the case of one Chandler man, 43-year-old Dwayne Meyers, who was president and CEO of a small community bank. He seemed to have it all: a great position that afforded him designer suits, a beautiful wife, two adorable children—but Meyers was one of many bankers over-lending to developers who had few assets. These developers were buying land and starting questionable commercial and residential projects. Meyers' bank, which is no longer in business, was in trouble.

But on May 20, 1985, Meyers disappeared. At first, police thought he took off because he was overextended and wanted to avoid mounting debts. Even when a ransom call was received three days later, police remained skeptical, suspecting Meyers was faking the kidnapping to get money. His bank put up the sum requested and dropped it off at the specified location. The money was taken, but something happened and police missed the pickup.

Then an unknown caller gave a location where to find Meyers. But when police arrived at the abandoned warehouse, Meyers was dead—found tied to a chair, his hands, ankles and mouth bound with duct tape. Police say he had been murdered at close range, with two gunshots to the head and one in the heart. No trace of the killer or killers has ever been found.

Now with new advancements in forensic technology, Chandler Police are resubmitting certain evidence for testing. They hope it will reveal clues to find those responsible for Meyers' death—and bring closure to his family.

If you have any information on this case, you are asked to call Chandler Police at 480-555-1000 or call Silent Witness at 1-800-555-9999. You may remain anonymous.

Reporting for KWLF-FM, I'm Lisa Powers.

I print out two copies, and deliver one set of stories to Grant's desk, smiling at him as I put them in his IN basket. I take the other set and slip them into a wall file folder marked NEWS next to the control room door.

"It's confirmed!" I shout across the newsroom to Grant.

I click "print" on my computer and take the sheet to his desk.

"Chandler PD says dental records confirm the deceased in the fire as Rosemary Thornton," I note. "No big surprise, but we still need to report on that development, right?"

Grant scans the document. "Yeah. Anything else new?"

"I'm gonna see if I can talk to the medical examiner about the autopsy, but not for this story. Do you want the identification separate from the backgrounder I'm doing on her, or together with it?"

"Doesn't sound like there's enough for a stand-alone on the ID. Include it in your lead-in to the story for now."

I turn to go back to my desk, but Grant asks, "What's the latest on the cold case?"

"Oh, that's what I've been meaning to talk to you about," I turn back apprehensively. "Chandler PD found the ex-wife in Sedona, and I thought—"

"Can you go up there to get an interview with her? That would be good," Grant says as I stop, stunned. "Was there something else?" he adds.

"Uh, well, um, yeah, actually," I stutter. "In the missing dad case, the son and daughter just don't think the police are doing enough, so they are going to try to retrace his steps tomorrow morning to see if they can find him. Maybe—"

"See if you can go along with them on the way to Sedona. Would be good reporter involvement in the story," Grant added. "Can you make it up there and back in one day? I'd let you take the live truck, but we need it at the statehouse tomorrow for a hearing, so you'll have to take your own car. Maybe Ron Thompson will go with you? Keep track of your receipts and the station'll pay for meals and gas."

I am nearly speechless, but manage to eke out, "Great, thanks," as I head back to my computer. I turn to look at Grant again, blinking a couple of times to make sure what just happened really happened, and he's already talking on the phone at his desk. I pull out Tyler Jameson's phone number obtained from Janet's cell phone and dial it.

"Yeah?" an irritated male voice answers.

"Is this Tyler Jameson?" I ask.

"Who's this?"

"I'm Lisa Powers from KWLF, and first let me say I am very sorry for your loss. I would just like—"

"I have no comment. You media types are all alike. Swarming around like vultures."

"Honestly, Mr. Jameson, that is not my intent. I'd like to do a story about Rosemary and all the philanthropic causes she was involved in. Would you—?"

"I don't know about half of what she did. Look on the web. I'm trying to plan a funeral. I gotta go."

"We would be happy to help let people know about when the services are. Do you have a date and time?"

"Saturday. 10 o'clock. Sun Valley."

"Thanks, perhaps we can talk at a later date about your wife?"

"I don't think so."

"Where were you the night of the—?"

There's a click and the call ends. *Well!* I take a breath and start to write:

ANCHOR LEAD-IN:

Police confirm the identity of the woman who died in that massive house fire Tuesday as 58-year-old Rosemary Thornton, heir to the Thornton Pharmaceutical Company. There's no cause of the fire yet, and an autopsy will be conducted. But as Lisa Powers reports, Thornton's life was charmed—yet full of contradictions:

LISA VO:

She was crowned Miss Indiana in her 20s, but in her later years, Rosemary Thornton rarely wore any make-up, other than her signature red lipstick and red fingernail polish.

She was next in line to inherit the multi-million-dollar Thornton Pharmaceutical Company, however Rosemary regularly saw a naturopathic physician.

She reportedly took herbal supplements, but was a heavy smoker.

She volunteered for numerous nonprofits over the past ten years, helping raise thousands and thousands of dollars—yet her neighbors had few positive things to say about her.

NEIGHBOR #1 SOT:

"I guess it's not polite to talk about someone after they're gone, but she wasn't the friendliest neighbor. I can't tell you how many times she'd leave her garbage can out in the street for days after pickup, and she was always hosting loud parties late into the night."

LISA VO:

Another resident who lived next door said he rarely saw Thornton.

NEIGHBOR #2 SOT:

"She mostly kept to herself. But one day she appeared on my doorstep, accusin' me of spyin' on her or some such nonsense. I never did know what she was talkin' about."

LISA VO:

Yet, those who served with her on various charities, such as Nancy Longmore, applauded the woman's generosity:

NEIGHBOR #3 SOT:

"Rosemary was so giving when it came to helping others. If she couldn't find someone to help donate money to a cause, she would give it herself. We had such a turnaround in our organization once Rosemary got involved. She could be a tough negotiator, but she knew how to raise money."

LISA VO:

The medical examiner's office says an autopsy is scheduled, which police say is routine for a fire death. Lisa Powers, KWLF Radio.

ANCHOR TAG:

Still no word on the cause of the blaze, although Thornton's third husband, Tyler Jameson, 43—who was reportedly at Saguaro Lake at the time of the fire—is cooperating with officials to determine how it started. Jameson tells KWLF his wife's funeral will be Saturday morning at 10 at Sun Valley Cemetery in Chandler.

I save the story, print two copies and set them aside. I open the cold case file, find a number and punch it into my desk phone.

"Hi, is this George Ware?"

"Yeah, who's this?" a gruff voice answers.

"This is Lisa Powers from KWLF Radio, and I'm looking into an old case that I believe you worked on when you were with Chandler P.D. Can I ask you a few questions?"

"I s'pose, like what?"

"Great, thanks. This is the 1985 case of a bank executive, Dwayne Meyers, who was reportedly kidnapped, then after a ransom was paid, was found dead—"

"Hold on, I don't know nuthin' about that case."

My eyebrows go up a bit at his interruption. "But according to the file, you were the lead investigator on—"

"Lady, what happened to Bobby wasn't my fault."

"I'm sorry, sir, I certainly didn't mean to imply—"

"I just mind my own business, and try to keep my nose clean, ya know?"

"Of course. Look, you're retired now, and it was a long time ago. Come on, let me buy you a drink and—"

"This ain't a good time, I gotta go," he mumbles.

"Okay, how about if I call you back this weekend to—" A startled expression comes over my face. I look down at the phone as the line is disconnected, and slowly hang up.

Jeez, twice in a row. A little rattled, I get up to look and listen to the Associated Press radio news feed, and its matching computer-generated story on the same monitor. I'm scrolling through the stories when I hear David at the back door.

"Lisa! You gotta come here, quick!"

I look up and see the truck engineer with a big grin on his face.

"What's going on?"

"Out here. See for yourself!"

We go outside, and David leads me behind the dumpster, in a corner where an old cardboard box sits amidst other rubbish.

"Shh..." David warns.

I peer inside the box at three of the tiniest little kittens I have ever seen.

"Oh, my goodness, they're adorable," I whisper. "Where's the momma?"

"I don't know, haven't seen her lately. You think she's still around?"

"I hope so, for their sake," I answer. "Let's keep an eye on them, and if the mother doesn't come back, well, we'll have to figure out something."

"*We,* kemosabe? My wife would kill me if I brought a cat home."

"Okay, okay, *I* will work it out."

I fill up the bowls and bring them to the box, calling for the mother. But I get no response.

I go back to my desk and once again pick up the fire file. I place a finger to mark a number, pick up the phone again and dial.

"Hello, is this Janet?"

A much more subdued voice on the other end answers.

"Yes. Who is this?"

"It's Lisa from KWLF radio. How are you feeling today?"

There's a pause. "I'm...fine. Why do you ask?"

Now it's my turn to stop. "Um, we met at O'Toole's yesterday, and I took you home? You had quite a bit to drink."

"Oh." Janet sounds downright meek. "I wasn't sure who...did you come up to my place?"

Shoot, I hope she doesn't suspect I took the white powder.

"Well, yes, just long enough to get you into bed, that's all. Hey, you talked about someone named 'Ty.' Who's that?"

Janet hesitates again. "Um, I, uh, I don't know any Ty. What did I say about him?"

"Oh, not much, just that you wanted to talk to him, but you couldn't reach him."

"Oh. I think you misunderstood. I was talking about...a *guy* I was trying to call. Not Ty, just a guy, no big deal. Did I say anything else?"

"Oh, no, you went right to sleep. Do you know Tyler Jameson, Rosemary Thornton's husband?"

Another long pause. "Uh, just in passing. Lisa, I...I am so sorry you saw me in that condition, and I'm very appreciative. I'd like to stop by and bring you a little something. Can I swing by your place tomorrow?"

I realize this might be a chance to get the powder packet back in my purse.

"Oh, you don't have to bring me a thing, but I would like to talk to you more about your volunteer work, maybe do a story on you. However, I'm going to be out of town on an assignment all day tomorrow. How about Saturday?"

"A story...about me?" Janet perks up. "Oh, well, that would be very nice. How's Saturday morning?"

"Um, I believe Rosemary Thornton's funeral service is Saturday morning at 10. Aren't you going?"

"Oh, gosh, I...it just slipped my mind. Of course, I'll be there. How about around 1?"

"Great." I give her the address and hang up, wondering how I will slip the powder back into Janet's purse without her knowing.

It's after 5, and I gather up my belongings to leave. As I walk away, my desk phone rings. I consider letting it go to voicemail, but change my mind, putting down my things to pick up the handset.

"Hi, this is Lisa."

"Chuck Douglas, returning your call."

"Oh, yes, Dr. Douglas, thanks for getting back with me." I hit record on the phone and dig out the file on the fire.

"I understand the Rosemary Thornton autopsy was scheduled for today, is that correct?"

"Well, it was, but we got behind, so it will be first thing in the morning."

"Oh, I see. What will you be looking for specifically?"

"I can't speak about this particular case yet, but in any routine death by fire, we will do the standard screening, which includes organs and a toxicology report."

"Um, I'm sorry if this is a morbid question, but how much of the body is left to autopsy after a fire?"

"Again, I can't release details yet, but as you can imagine, the skin and flesh, which are mostly water, usually burn away. However, typically the internal organs and bones are usually in remarkably decent shape to autopsy. Now, if there's nothing else—"

"Just one more question. When will you have your report completed?"

"Unlike those crime shows, it usually takes a couple of months to get all the results back from the various labs involved. So, about eight weeks is normal, longer if other circumstances show up."

"Circumstances like what?"

"Like any abnormalities or unusual findings. Now, I really have to go."

"Thank you, I apprec—" but the line is already dead. *Third time's a charm,* I think to myself.

As I leave the station, I go around back to check on the kitties.

"Pretty momma, where are you?" I call as I tiptoe behind the trash receptacle. The kittens are huddled together in the box, but there's no sign of the mother. Worse yet, both bowls are still full. I find an old piece of T-shirt in the rubbish and gently tuck it around the kitties.

"Hang in there, little ones..."

The murder mystery podcast theme music fades in, and my voice begins.

"Welcome back once again to 'Murder in the Air Mystery Theatre.' I'm Lauren Price. In the Frightful Fun House, our carnival couple, Brad and Liz, slid down a long dark chute into a ball pit, and are now desperately trying to get out. What could be behind the door that says 'Insanitorium?'"

"C'mon, Liz, that looks like the only exit," Brad says as he pulls Liz toward the large door, slipping and sliding on the balls.

"I don't know, Brad. What's an Insanitorium anyway?" Liz asks nervously.

"It's probably...oh heck, it's just a name to get us freaked out!" Brad reaches for the doorknob.

"Well, they're doing a good job of it!"

The knob turns, and the door creaks open slowly as Brad and Liz peer into a large dark room.

"I don't see anything, Liz," Brad says. "Looks like it's empty."

They inch through the door. It slams shut behind them with a loud bang.

"What the—?" Brad begins, but is interrupted when a light comes on behind a portion of the wall, showing a clear glass partition. Something—or someone—is inside.

"Brad, what...who...is that?"

A scratchy old recording of carnival music begins slowly, finally getting up to normal speed. A male voice follows.

"Laaaa-dies aaaaand gentlemennn...step right up...for the most unbelievable...truly unusual...but absolutely real human oddities you have ever seen..."

A young boy with an enormously distended face steps forward toward the glass. He has a huge mass of skin growing in the right side of his face that reaches down to his waist. His right eye is buried under the extra folds of flesh, nodules, lumps and growths.

"Oh, my god," Liz whispers.

"Ladies and gentlemen...let me introduce you to Elephant Boy. He suffers from a rare hereditary disorder that used to be known as 'elephantiasis,' but is now known as Proteus syndrome. It results in overgrown skin, an abnormally large head, giant feet and darkened moles on the skin. Because of the size and weight of his head—estimated to be about 23 pounds—he must always sleep sitting up. If he doesn't, the weight of his head will crush his windpipe and suffocate him...to death."

The boy steps back away from the glass, and the light goes out.

"We gotta look for another way out, Liz. See if you—" Brad begins, but the male voice begins an added tale as a light illuminates yet another partition across the room. A woman with four legs and four arms and a second torso is seated in a chair.

"Hindu goddess? Or skeletal abnormality? Makeesha was born with four legs, four arms and a headless torso—extra limbs from a parasitic twin that never developed properly..."

"Brad! I can't take this! How do we get out of here?"

"I don't know, Liz, I don't see how—"

Again, the light goes out. Across the room, another light comes on, but this time, the partition is empty and Brad and Liz see a body lying crumpled on the floor in front of the glass. The carny voice begins, but the tape sounds like it's warped, running at different speeds.

"Trrrrrrrreeeeee maaaaaaan is a grotesque sight to see. His arms and legs aaaaaaarrrrrrrre covered with woody growths. It's an out...control...viruuuuuussssss..." The voice slows and goes down in pitch before fading out.

"Brad, that looks like...it's a woman...I think she's...dead!"

"Is it just another diabolical sideshow freak? Or have Liz and Brad discovered the victim of a horrendous crime? Stay tuned next time for another podcast of 'Murder in the Air Mystery Theatre.' Thanks for listening...this is Lauren Price."

Chapter 5

FRIDAY, APRIL 12

We take the Cordes Junction exit off north Interstate 17, where, in the distance, Paolo Soleri's Arcosanti is nestled on the desert cliff. I recall doing a story on the famous architect just before his death in 2013 at age 94, and always think about my first sale of a news story to NPR, covering a huge fire during a concert there. Afterwards, the cars destroyed in the blaze were buried across the gravel road. I realize the olive trees planted in a sculpture garden over the auto entombment have grown since the last time I was there.

As I drive, the details of the Soleri story flow through my mind. The groundbreaking designer, who was also an artist, craftsman and philosopher, based the project on the theory of compact city design, as an alternative to urban sprawl. My account told of some 7,000 volunteers who helped build Arcosanti starting in 1970, and people still live, work, visit and take part in educational and cultural programs. *If I had more time, I'd like to volunteer there.*

Ron and I join Joan and her brother, Jerry, a tall, beefy, no-nonsense 40-something, at the McDonald's. We sip coffee and pour over maps stretched out on the table. The morning sun shines brightly through the tall windows, and the restaurant is abuzz with breakfast diners.

"So, I...we were wondering, what if your dad didn't take the interstate?" I ask.

Jerry and Joan look at each other with curiosity.

"Well, I suppose that's possible, but he always went up I-17 and took the Camp Verde exit," Joan replies.

"But maybe after stopping here, he decided to take the scenic route towards Prescott then through Jerome. Have you ever driven those winding roads?"

"Well, no. Are they bad?"

"They can be. I think it's worth checking out."

"Well, maybe we go up that way, then come back down I-17." Jerry nods grimly in acceptance.

I fold up the map. "That sounds like a plan. Follow me."

The two vehicles, with Ron and I in the lead, head northwest on Highway 69 on the back roads toward Prescott and Sedona.

"Hey, Ron, remember when this was a terrible, curvy two-lane highway?"

"And how. Haven't been up this way for years."

I steer my car easily on the upgraded four-lane asphalt through the sleepy little towns of Mayer, Dewey and Humboldt. We go past Albertson Farms, the site of many seasonal events.

"I did a story last October on pumpkin festivals, and included this place. Look at all that sweet corn. Maybe we'll stop and pick some up on the way home."

We continue on the paved road as it gently winds around the rolling hills dotted with small houses.

I wonder how I could pitch Grant on a story about this area of the state. Maybe in June, when the Valley heats up and residents want to escape to the cooler mountain towns like Prescott, known for its pine trees and four distinct, moderate seasons.

"Didn't you cover a trial in Prescott once?" Ron stretches out his legs and leans his seat back.

"Yep. It was a Chandler man accused of robbing and killing a convenience store owner. The trial got moved to Prescott on a change of venue, and I got to stay up there for a week. It was beautiful. The old county courthouse in the downtown square reminded me of the ones I grew up with in Iowa."

Signs for the Prescott Country Club appear ahead.

"Don't let me miss the exit," I say.

Ron looks at the map, then the highway. "It should be the next right."

I check my rear view mirror to make sure Joan and Jerry are still behind us. At the intersection, the caravan exits onto Fain Road, which takes them east of Prescott Valley. Within a few minutes, we're on the flat, level two-lane 89A, heading nearly directly east.

The day is clear, but at this early hour, the rising sun just above Mingus Mountain is almost blinding. I lower my car's sun visor.

"Are you thinking what I'm thinking?" I ask, as I shield my eyes against the bright glare.

Ron simply nods in agreement, adjusting his visor as well.

Within about 11 miles, the terrain suddenly changes from dry, flat desert and scrub brush to more mountainous, with thick trees on either side of the road. The straight pavement begins curving in all directions.

"Make sure your seatbelt's good and tight, Ron," I admonish as I take the first turn. "And keep your eyes peeled."

As we head deeper into pine country, the switchbacks become more intense, forcing our speed down to 15 miles an hour or less.

After one particularly hairy series of curves, Ron shouts, "Pull over!"

As I turn the car off the pavement and onto the gravel, with Joan and Jerry behind us, Ron simply points. The end of a guardrail has been knocked over and is twisted and bent. However, not one, but two sets of tire tracks veer off the highway into the trees.

Joan, Jerry and I rush out of our cars, following the impressions in the sandy soil.

"Ron, stay here and call 9-1-1!" I yell back, as I head to the side of the road.

"Hello! Anyone down there?" I call out.

Joan and Jerry scream for their father.

"Dad! Dad! Can you hear me?"

The tracks head down into a ravine, showing a swath of felled trees about the same width as a car.

"Help...help me!" comes a weak male voice.

"We found him!" Jerry screams. "I'm going down!"

"Wait a minute, I've got some gear that will help." I run back to the car, reach into the vehicle's trunk and grab a long rope, a blanket and a water bottle. Tying the cord to my bumper, I toss part of it to Jerry, who starts down the hill. I attach the water bottle to my waist, press the digital record button and sling my recorder and the blanket over my shoulder and follow him.

"Dad, we're coming!" Jerry is huffing with exertion through the thick brambles. Sharp thorns snag my clothes, and the dry brush crackles under my feet, sending up small clouds of brown dust.

Jerry reaches the bottom, and his eyes well up with tears when he finds his father in a crumpled heap amidst thick plants, cactus and broken car parts.

"You...you're here, son. I knew you'd find me," Mark Rogers says in a tired, raspy voice.

When I climb down, Jerry is holding his dad's hand and gently stroking his head.

"Thank god we found you, Dad. You're going to be just fine."

I bend down beside them, offering the water bottle.

"Hi, Mr. Rogers, I'm Lisa. Here's a little water, but don't drink too fast."

I help the man lift his head and hold the bottle so a small flow reaches his parched lips.

"Ahh...tastes...so good," Mark Rogers says with a tired smile.

I arrange the blanket over the man, and bunch one end into a small pillow under his head.

"We need to wait for help, but they'll be here soon," I say reassuringly.

I get to my feet, relieved the man is still alive. But elation turns to horror when I make another gruesome discovery: the spot where the second set of tire tracks ends.

ANNOUNCER LEAD-IN:
Amazing news in the case of the missing Chandler father. Almost a week after he disappears, his crashed car is found—and he is alive. Lisa Powers has the story from the scene:

LISA VO:
It was the determination and perhaps sheer stubbornness of 67-year-old Mark Rogers' adult children who discovered their dad at the bottom of a ravine after his car plunged down the side of a cliff off the winding and treacherous road from Prescott to Jerome.

He left Chandler early last Sunday morning to go bird watching with friends in Clarkdale, but never made it. His daughter, Joan Rogers-Hartley and her brother Jerry, took matters into their own hands—even consulting psychics after expressing frustration with police who they felt weren't working hard enough to find their father. Rogers-Hartley explains what happened:

SOT: JOAN ROGERS-HARTLEY

"Lisa convinced us to try a route where he normally might not have gone. We found an area on a really twisting hairpin section of road where we saw tire tracks and started calling until we heard 'Help me!'"

LISA VO W/ SFX OF NAT SOUND UNDER:

They called 9-1-1, but Jerry wasn't about to wait.

SOT: JERRY HARTLEY

"Dad, we're coming!"

NATSOT of dry brush crackling under footsteps, Jerry huffing and puffing down the hill.

LISA VO W/ SFX OF NAT SOUND UNDER:

He and this reporter went slipping and sliding down the steep slope of the mountain to get to his father. We found Mark Rogers thrown from his car—dehydrated and bloody, and with broken bones—but able to say, "I knew you'd find me."

But there's a grim twist: Rogers' vehicle was found near another car that had gone off in the exact same spot. Unfortunately, that driver, a man in his 80s, did not make it. Police say he had been reported missing three weeks ago.

But for the Rogers family, they are grateful to have found their dad.

SOT: JOAN ROGERS-HARTLEY

"We are so excited and so thankful to have him back and alive."

LISA VO:

Joan says her dad will spend a few days in Yavapai Regional Medical Center recuperating from broken ribs, a broken leg and various cuts and scratches—but doctors say he is expected to make a full recovery. From mile marker 107, outside Jerome, I'm Lisa Powers, KWLF News.

Ron and I wave as the ambulance carrying Mark Rogers and his daughter head south toward the Valley, followed by Jerry in his car.

"That was pretty amazing, huh?" I smile. But when I glance at my friend, he is looking a bit gray in the face. "Ron, are you okay? Let's get you in the car."

With his oxygen levels adjusted, Ron's color comes back, and I pull out onto the winding road.

"Maybe we should forget Sedona and go back to Phoenix." *The last thing I want is for Ron to get sick, or worse.*

"No, I'm fine," Ron assures me. "In all the excitement, I just took off my air for longer than I should've. Let's go see some red rocks," he says with a smile.

"We'll be there in time to have a late lunch at Shaker's Cafe," I grin.

"I sure hope you brought a change of clothes," Ron admonishes, eyeing my muddy and torn pants.

After calling in the story to the station, it's a quiet ride on the back roads through Clarkdale and Cottonwood to the majestic red rock mountains of Sedona, with Ron and me deep in our own thoughts.

Let's see, if I write about Sedona, it might start something like: 'Known worldwide for its vortexes, crystals and sweat lodges, Sedona is also a popular retirement area for the wealthy, tourist attraction for people from around the globe.' I could also include a little about the many art galleries and upscale resorts.

Driving through the Coconino National Forest, we pass regal pine trees, prickly pear and agave cactus with scrub brush on either side of the road. Yellow and white daisies push up alongside orange and brown flowers along Highway 89-A coming into West Sedona, which avoids the multiple controversial roundabouts through the Village of Oak Creek on the main route from I-17. Ron points out the Red Rock State Park on the right, and a little later, the Sedona Performing Arts Center near Sedona High.

At the restaurant, I now sport a fresh purple polo shirt with clean khaki pants, spares I keep in my car. We indulge our healthy appetites, with Ron downing Lobster Green Chile Mac & Cheese and me enjoying Mamma's Meatloaf at the popular eatery.

I catch my older friend dozing on the way to our appointment, and I feel guilty, thinking I am pushing him too hard. But the catnap seems to energize Ron, who suddenly opens his eyes just a couple of miles away.

"So, this ex, Denise, she was okay with us comin' to see her?" Ron asks.

"Well, not at first. It took a little convincing."

A few moments go by as we both ponder the reason for her reluctance.

"Maybe she feels guilty for divorcing the guy, then he ends up dead," I remark.

"Maybe she has something to hide," Ron adds.

The drive takes Ron and me past gated communities with massive Santa Fe-style adobe homes and beautiful sprawling mansions of the well to do, the ever-present red rocks all around.

"With that kind of insurance money, I bet Denise's got a gorgeous place up here," I tell Ron, who has a map spread on his lap. "You sure you don't want me to plug in the address to my GPS?"

"Nah, nothing like a good ol' paper map to get you where you wanna go. Just keep heading west."

We drive a little farther, and the homes on either side become smaller and less ostentatious. We keep going, and the paved road turns into dirt. Unattended dry grass and scrub brush give the area a forgotten feel.

"Uh, you sure about this, Ron?" I ask with a frown.

"Says 3825 Red Rock Drive, and we just passed the 3600 block. I think we're close. Look, could that be it?"

The older man points to a mobile home park with the address 3800 Red Rock Drive. He and I exchange a glance, and I pull into the entrance. A few yards down the road is 3825. It's a cream-colored manufactured home, or what is referred to as a "double wide," with more mobile homes on either side of it in a long row. Many have flags, garden gnomes, light catchers, name plates and other garden "art," but 3825 is very plain, and looks neglected.

"Wow, not quite what I expected," I say, stopping the car. "Let me make sure this is the right place."

I walk onto round, gray concrete stepping-stones to the porch, go up the short steps and knock on the door. Slowly, two locks *clack* as they are unlatched.

A striking woman with high cheekbones and long, pale blonde hair streaked with gray answers the door, peering through the security chain lock.

"Mrs. Richardson?" I ask.

"Yes?" Dwayne Meyers' ex-wife looks warily at me.

"I'm Lisa with KWLF."

Denise cautiously removes the chain, looking up and down the street and at Ron in my car.

"It's very nice to meet you," I say. "A good friend of mine made the trip with me. Is it okay if he comes in as well?" I motion to Ron.

Denise watches him suspiciously at first, and visibly relaxes when she sees his oxygen tank. "Of course," she says as she opens the door, letting us in. I note that Denise locks it quickly behind us, before guiding us through the narrow entryway and into a small combination living room and kitchen. The house has only the basics of furnishings—an old sofa, a recliner, an end table with lamp and a kitchen table with two chairs. The area is devoid of any wall art, and little in the way of decor except for a couple of framed photos. Children's crayon art covers a small refrigerator.

"I made some sun tea. Would you like a glass?" she offers.

Once Ron and I settle on the sofa, Denise, looking nervous, takes the slim recliner across from us. Her legs, crossed at the ankles, are tucked under the chair, and her arms rest in a defensive position across her chest. She wears no make-up, but is nearly as beautiful as her earlier photo, just with a few crow's feet around her blue eyes.

I put a small audio recorder on the coffee table between them.

"Oh, I didn't know this was going to be taped," Denise interjects, putting her arms out in front of her as if pushing away the device.

"It's for your own protection, Mrs. Richardson, so I make sure to get all the information correct," I assure her.

"Oh, I see. I guess that's all right then." She crosses her arms again and begins rocking the chair nervously.

"So, Mrs. Richardson—"

"Call me Denise, please."

"Thanks, Denise. So take us back to 1985. Tell us a little about your life with Dwayne Meyers."

There's a pause as one of Denise's hands flutters to her face, where she absently rubs her cheek.

"Well, 1985 was a terrible year in many ways. Before that, though, we were relatively happy. We had two beautiful children, and my husband—ex-husband—was a successful businessman. We traveled and the children were involved in a lot of activities. In about 1983 Dwayne was named CEO and president of the Santan Community Bank."

"So, the bank was doing well financially?"

"For the first couple of years, yes. But after that, Dwayne started lending to developers who were buying a lot of land. Some of the board members were afraid the deals were too risky, that these so-called developers really didn't have any collateral of their own. But Dwayne kept going until the bank got into trouble. That was when I started divorce proceedings. I just couldn't believe he was throwing away our security and our children's stability."

"What happened the day he disappeared?"

Denise closes her eyes as if to summon extra strength.

"He was living in an apartment nearby, and I had talked to him that morning, something to do with the kids. He was on his way to work, and seemed a little on edge, but it was nothing too unusual for those times. But when his secretary called around 11 to ask if I knew where he was, I had a horrible feeling something was wrong. When I didn't hear anything from him by evening, I called the police."

"What did they say?"

Denise uncrosses her arms and legs and leans forward toward me.

"At first, they thought he took off to avoid all the debts we were facing," she says with disgust. "But when the first ransom call came in two days later, I knew we were up against something much worse."

"I understand the police suspected your husband had perhaps faked the ransom call to get the money himself, is that right?"

"Yes, but that was ridiculous. Dwayne would never do that."

"Did Dwayne own Armani suits?" I ask.

The question takes Denise somewhat by surprise. She blinks a couple of times.

"Oh, well, yes, I believe he had a couple of them. He was a handsome man, and a community leader." As if she needed to defend him.

"Of course," I reply. "So, the bank puts up the ransom, $1.5 million, right?"

"Yes, which was a lot of money in 1985. But after the police dropped off the cash at the specified location, somehow they screwed it up and missed catching the guys when they picked it up. The cops said something about 'being outnumbered,' but I never believed 'em. They got away, and afterwards police found Dwayne." Her eyes fill with tears. Obviously, the emotions still rub raw nearly 30 years later.

"Why do you think they killed Dwayne, when they got the money, too?"

"I...really don't know," Denise says, rocking nervously in her chair again. Ron and I look at each other, wondering if she is not telling the whole story.

"Did Dwayne ever wear shoes without socks?" I ask.

Denise stops and looks hard at me, brow furrowed.

"What? Oh, well, come to think of it, I guess he did sometimes."

"Did Dwayne drink or do drugs?"

There's a long pause. Denise gets up and walks toward a large plate glass window covered with a thick curtain. She pushes back a bit of the drapery and peeks out onto the desert behind the house, her shoulders slumping.

"You'll have to turn that recorder off now." Her voice was soft, dejected.

"Why?"

"Because I've never shared this with anyone, not even my own children." She waited until I complied.

Denise paused and took a big breath. "He...there was another reason why I wanted out of the marriage," Denise begins. "The whole savings-and-loan mess, the financial problems, even his attitude that everything was just fine, I could've lived with. But..."

"He was doing something you hated." Ron made it sound like a statement rather than a question.

"Yes," Denise whispered. "But I've never told a soul. I couldn't tell anyone, and I never told the police." Tears begin to flow down her fair cheeks.

"What is it?" I ask quietly.

"He was...taking...oh God, he was...on heroin."

Silence hangs in the air as Ron and I absorb the news. We look at each other in surprise.

"Heroin? Are you sure, Denise?" I ask.

Denise snickers through her tears. "He said he found it relaxing, and that he liked it better than drinking alcohol." She shakes her head. "No one knew. Not his friends, not anyone at the bank, not even his family. And you can't tell them!" Denise turns suddenly, imploring them with her eyes. "They...would be devastated."

"But Denise, is it possible that Dwayne owed money to drug dealers? Maybe it didn't have anything to do with the bank at all."

Denise paused, and looked down to the right, halting eye contact. "I...no, it couldn't be. He said he didn't do it that much."

I catch the sign of a potential lie in her body language, and decide to change the subject slightly.

"Heroin is a highly addictive drug, Denise. Did he complain of muscle pain, or was he ever restless and couldn't sleep at night?"

"Sure, he had insomnia a lot, but I figured it was because he was worried about the bank."

"Those are also symptoms of withdrawal from heroin, which may have happened between the times he was using," I explain.

"You asked about his not wearing socks," Denise adds. "He would inject that damned stuff between his toes so no one would see needle marks."

Standing at the door, ready to leave, I do my best to convince Denise to tell police about her ex-husband's heroin addiction.

"It could really make the difference in solving this case once and for all," I say.

"Yeah, and your kids are all grown up now. They'd understand," Ron adds.

"Please, I don't know, let me think about it, I—"

Suddenly, a car races down the small street outside the mobile home, spewing gravel. A gunshot rings out.

"What the—?" Ron says, ducking.

"Get down!" I scream, grabbing Denise and pulling her to the floor.

Another shot rings as it hits the metal door. Tires squeal and the car fishtails as it leaves as fast as it arrived.

I open the door a crack, and peer out from the floor.

"It's a black four-door...but I can't see the license plate."

"Who would do this?" Ron demands. "Is there something else you're not telling us?"

Denise sits up against the wall, eyes wide with fear. "It's them," she whispers.

"It's who, Denise?!" I hiss. "Tell us! You know who they are!"

It's late Friday night back at Chandler Police headquarters. Sergeant Hoffman and Detective Johnstone sit stone-faced around the conference table with Ron and me and the cold case file boxes. They listen to Denise, tears streaking her face, telling her story, including her ex-husband's drug use, and this time revealing being terrorized for years by an unknown person—or persons.

A stack of papers spills out of an open shoebox, its lid to the side. Johnstone picks up one page, which has letters cut out of newspaper and magazines to spell "leave $5k under the matt. dont tell anywon."

"At first, they arrived every couple of weeks. Sometimes in the mail, sometimes under the front door, sometimes on my car windshield. They always knew where I was. Even when I moved to Southern California, they found me. But the notes and letters came less frequently, until it was only about once a year, around...around the time of Dwayne's death."

Denise pauses, and breaks into sobs.

"I know this is difficult for you, Mrs. Richardson," starts Hoffman. "But why didn't you tell police? We could've put surveillance on you, your house, and we might have caught them."

Denise looks through the stack of papers until she finds what she's looking for. She hands the sheet to Hoffman.

"He...they threatened to kill my children," she said softly, between sniffles.

"'Tell anywon and yor kids are dead,'" Hoffman reads.

There's a long pause in the room.

"You s'pose they tapped her phones? That's how they knew we were comin' to see her?" Ron asks.

"It's very likely," Johnstone replies.

"I'm so sorry, Denise," I begin. But Denise waves her hand, shaking her head as she blows her nose with a tissue.

"No, it's long past time. They've drained me of nearly everything I had. I know I should've said something sooner, but now I have grandchildren," she sobs again, her eyes pleading as she looks at everyone at the table. "You have to keep them all safe, you just have to!"

Johnstone nods his head. "We'll do everything we can. Sedona P.D. is keeping an eye on your house, and Phoenix has around-the-clock protection on your children and their families. I'm going to send those notes to an FBI guy who knows forensic linguistics. Meanwhile, we'd like you to stay at a safe location here in Chandler until we get a line on these guys."

"Of course, whatever you say." She pauses again, this time letting out a long sigh. "Maybe it will really be over soon."

A female police officer leads Denise out of the conference room door. Ron and I stay behind, anxious to talk to Hoffman and Johnstone alone.

"So, any luck with fingerprints?" I ask.

Hoffman pulls a sheet out of the manila folder in front of him. "Not yet, but I found the investigator in Texas you told me about who got prints off the frozen tape, and have sent him what we have. If he can't find anything, I'll get the duct tape to the lab in Florida that used the ultraviolet light in the Casey Anthony case."

"Sgt. Hoffman, do you know if there is a recording of the original ransom call?"

"I'm sure there is, but I don't know what format it's in." He looks through a paper file, and digs into one of the Meyers' case evidence boxes, coming up with a quarter-inch reel-to-reel audiotape.

"Joe, maybe you could send it along with the ransom notes to that FBI expert?"

"Sure," he says, making a note. "Oh, and ballistics didn't find anything different from the old bullets, but now we've got new ones to check," Johnstone adds, looking encouraged. "I s'pose you'd like to sit in on that?"

"Sure, thanks! And how about the DNA testing?" I ask hopefully.

"Now, you know it's only on TV that those tests come back so fast. In real life, it can take six to eight weeks or longer." Johnstone pauses, smiling. "But with the latest developments, we might be able to put a rush on them."

I grin at Ron and the older man gives me a wink.

"Hey, don't look so pleased, young lady. Didja forget that there are a couple of really bad dudes out there who now know exactly what kind of car you drive?"

Our faces drop. "You gotta keep an eye on Lisa here, too," Ron says gruffly.

"We will do our best. But you both need to be vigilant. Watch where you go, and don't do anything foolish."

"Of course, Detective," I say solemnly. I raise one eyebrow. "But maybe you can set up a sting with me and my car? You know, I drive somewhere, park and we try to trap them—"

"Now, what did I just say?" Johnstone interrupts. "*If* we thought it was a viable plan, and *if* we decide to do such an operation, we have guidelines about these things, and it would only be with an undercover officer who is trained in these procedures." He pauses. "But a sting might be a good idea," he concedes.

"I'll take you home, Ron, but I gotta check one thing at the station first." It's been a long day, and we're both bushed.

"Geez, it's nearly midnight, can't it wait 'til tomorrow?"

"Sorry, it really can't. I promise it won't take long."

We drive to the radio station, and I park near the dumpster, leaving the engine running. "You stay here, I'll just be a minute."

I find a flashlight in my glove compartment, and shine it on the ground. It flashes on the bowls—still full. My heart sinks. I move the beam to the box, and kneel down. I remove the piece of fabric, still in the same spot, and smile when I see the kittens.

"Oh, you sweet little things, what happened to your momma?" I whisper. I reach down to pet one, but it's stiff, and still. *Oh no, it's dead! Damn it!* I tentatively touch the other two to find them alive, but with eyes still shut and barely breathing. "You're coming with me," I say, as I pick up the box and head back to the car.

The "'Murder in the Air Mystery Theatre" theme music fades up and under, as my voice begins:

"The Frightful Fun House lost its sense of humor long ago—and Brad and Liz desperately attempt to find a way out. However, they've been stuck in an Insanitorium, where sideshow freaks are on display. The freak show comes to an end when our carnival couple discovers an unconscious woman beside the glass."

"Is she...I mean, do you think...?" Liz and Brad creep slowly toward the older woman immobile on the floor, whose hand appears to be clutching her throat. She's dressed in polyester pants and a sweatshirt, and has white curly hair. A walking cane lies not far from her body.

"On TV they always touch somewhere on the neck," Brad says quietly. *"But I'm not sure what they're feeling for."*

He gets down on his knees and bends over the woman to see if he can hear her breathing. He gently touches her hand, and retracts his own quickly.

"Oh, god, she's cold, Jesus Christ, I think she is...goddammit, we have to find help and get out of here!" Brad gets up and bangs on the clear glass. He starts pushing on all the glass panels.

"Help! We need help here!" Liz screams.

"Hey!" Brad yells, but his voice disappears. Liz looks around and can't find him.

"Brad? Where did you go? Brad!"

Suddenly, it's only Liz and the dead woman in the room.

As the "Murder in the Air Mystery Theatre" theme music fades up, my voice comes in:

"Has there been a murder, or did the Frightful Fun House scare this woman to death? And where did Brad disappear to—again? Join us again for another 'Murder in the Air Mystery Theatre.' I'm Lauren Price, thanks for listening."

CHAPTER 6

SATURDAY, APRIL 13

It's going to be a restless weekend staying inside my apartment.

After Chandler police impound my car, "for my own safety," I got a nondescript rental and Grant agreed the station should pay for it. He wanted me to take some additional time off, but I argued there were too many stories I still needed to cover.

Johnstone warned me to lie low for a few days, and sent a squad car around every shift for my protection. He said the department was short-staffed on the weekend and couldn't assign a round-the-clock security detail to me, but they would certainly know if I went somewhere in the leased vehicle.

Besides worrying how to return the packet of unknown white stuff to Janet, and the Thornton funeral, I expect it's going to be a quiet couple of days.

I spend some time on the Internet, looking into forensic linguistics as it applies to the cold case's verbal ransom call and the written demand notes sent to Denise. I smile when I learn that forensic linguistics and a free software program were used to "out" J.K. Rowling as the author of *The Cuckoo's Calling*, using the pen name "Robert Galbraith."

I find out a set of linguistic tools helps investigators analyze written and spoken communications such as letters, text messages, emails, voicemail messages or any other kind of communication to gain information about an author. I discover writers often try to "sound like" a street thug, for instance, and wonder if that was the case in the misspelled demand letters.

The two tiny kitties keep me somewhat occupied. The previous night I Googled "how to care for newborn kittens without mother" and got the babies warmed up with a heating pad and a thick towel in a little basket. The lady at the pet store recommended a high-fat kitten milk replacer, and with an eyedropper, I succeeded in squeezing some liquid into each of the babies every few hours. They started to move around a bit on their own, yet would never stray too far from each other. Both sported a mixture of black, brown and tan fur, but had individual markings on their little faces.

"You're gonna make it, little ones, then I'll find you a good home, don't worry."

I make arrangements to attend Rosemary's funeral by having a police officer chauffeur me to the Sun Valley Cemetery. A faint floral smell drifts through the door as I enter, and grows more intense from the dozens of huge flower bouquets filling the chapel.

Quite a crowd shows, considering some of the animosity toward the socialite. But it is more of a who's who affair than paying respects to the deceased. Women from various charity organizations are dressed to the hilt in their little black dresses and fancy black hats, and some pass by the closed mahogany casket in the front.

I take a seat towards the middle left so I can watch Thornton's husband, Tyler, sitting in the right front row by himself. He looks somewhat bored. *He's a handsome man,* I think, *but not looking the part of a grieving spouse.* He's not very tall, but his piercing blue eyes stood out in contrast to his dark, outdoor tan. He looks out of place in a dark tailored suit, and I assume he'd rather be wearing jeans, out fishing somewhere.

The bench in the front row on the opposite side is full, with various men looking stoic and a number of women clutching hankies as they dab their eyes.

The small program includes a color photo of Rosemary, staring back at me, steely-eyed with one raised eyebrow. The date below reads Feb. 1, 1949—April 9, 2013. Inside is the brief schedule, which includes a eulogy, followed by burial information and a post-funeral reception.

I watch as the last people come in and take their seats, and out of the corner of my eye, see Janet enter by herself. The diminutive woman gazes around, and looks for a place to sit. After a few seconds, Janet goes up the left side aisle past me and slips into the far end of the fourth row. The couple sitting there scoots over for her, with only a polite nodding of their heads.

I quietly press Record on my machine.

The organist finishes playing "The Old Rugged Cross," and the minister begins the service. I tune him out, thinking about Tyler. *Need to find out more about him. He's almost 20 years younger than her, and he's her third husband. Wonder if there was a pre-nup? Maybe he's a gold digger?*

I glance at Janet, and sees she's not paying attention to the preacher either, but is staring at Tyler with an odd, intense expression. *Is that anger?* I wonder. *Is there something going on between those two?*

A tall, elegant woman takes the podium.

"On behalf of everyone with the Friends of the Chandler Food Bank, we are deeply sorry to hear of Rosemary's passing. She was very involved in our organization, and could always be counted on to give generously when our shelves were bare. We hope that her dear husband, Tyler, will see fit to continue her good work."

The woman looks straight at Tyler, who is now wearing a weary look on his face, as if this wasn't the first pitch—or the last—he was going to hear.

A distinguished-looking man from the front row, wearing an expensive suit with a carefully folded burgundy handkerchief in his breast pocket, strides up to the front.

"Rosemary was a beloved member of the Thornton family, and of Thornton Pharmaceuticals," he says. *Not terribly sincere,* I muse. "We are saddened at her death, and while she was a member of the board of directors, we want to assure stockholders and employees that the company will continue as normal."

Good grief, is that all anyone can think of? Where's the love?

As the service ends, the family members in the front row are escorted to the lobby of the reception hall, and greet attendees with stiff hugs and teary eyes. I watch as Janet makes a beeline to Tyler, but he shakes his head firmly and walks away from her. A dark expression comes back to Janet's face as she whirls around and quickly stomps out of the room.

Looks like she knows Tyler Jameson well—very well, I think to myself.

I had planned to skip the interment, but decide I want to see if Janet and Tyler interact in any other way.

At the graveside ceremony, Janet stays way in the back as Tyler stands in the front near, but not next to, Rosemary's family. *Obviously a point of some contention there,* I believe, based on the stiff body language.

The beautiful mahogany casket, highly polished and gleaming in the spring sun, is slowly lowered into the ground. A little girl, wearing a frilly pink dress with matching headband and shoes, walks up and throws a pink rose onto the container that holds Rosemary's remains.

Back at the reception hall, a large room opens, filled with tables of expensive catered food and drink. People mill around, laughing and chatting, as if at a cocktail party.

Once again, I watch for Janet and Tyler. I see Rosemary's widowed husband in much higher spirits, talking to another man, both grinning and at ease. I spot Janet off to the side, clutching her purse tightly, and looking as if she's waiting for Tyler's conversation to end. When it doesn't in the time that Janet obviously wants it to, I watch as Janet finally approaches Tyler, a fake smile on her face. I move a little closer, but it's noisy in the room and I can't hear all of the conversation.

"Hello, Tyler, lovely service," I hear, watching as the man talking to Tyler pats him on the back and leaves. The smile on Janet's face fades quickly. "...haven't called...really need...speak with you about..."

Tyler scowls at the interruption, "Not here, not..." I catch. He grabs Janet by the elbow and steers her away, out of the room. I follow.

The pair goes into a room marked "Private" and closes the door. Trying to look casual, I take my drink and stand outside the room, bending my head slightly to see if I can hear anything.

"You promised!" I hear Janet's voice say loudly.

Tyler responds in a calmer, low voice, one that I perceive only as a rumble.

"Don't wait too long, or I swear, I'll..." Janet warns. She drops her voice too low for me to distinguish her words.

The minister walks by me with a smile and pauses.

"Very nice ceremony, Reverend."

He murmurs, "Thank you," and continues on his way. The door behind me starts to open, and I walk quickly back into the hall. I turn around just in time to see Janet walking off in a huff, leaving Tyler with a red face and deep frown.

Home at the apartment, while feeding the tiny felines again, my phone dings with a calendar reminder. *Janet will be here any minute.* I reach into my pants pocket and feel the baggie. Janet would have to leave her purse unattended for me to slip it in without her seeing. *And wouldn't she know later that it suddenly reappeared?* Maybe I could put it in Janet's pocket, and Janet would just think she misplaced it after being so drunk. *But what if she doesn't have a pocket to put it into? Oh, this is too frustrating!* I decide if it doesn't happen today, I'd have to figure out another time, and by then, maybe Ron's friend will have...

The doorbell rings, and I jump.

I open the door. "Hi, Janet," I say, gesturing for the short woman to come in. Janet is dressed in a more subdued pants and casual top showing less of her ample bosom than before. The only pockets are in her rather snug-fitting trousers. She's carrying the same purse as the other day, and it's slung over her shoulder.

I also notice Janet's hair has been cut rather badly on the front. She's holding a plate covered with aluminum foil.

"Hello, Lisa." Janet walks in and holds the plate out to me. "I brought you some of my rather famous chocolate chip cookies as a token of my thanks for...well, for the other day when I was certainly not acting my normally professional self. Will you please forgive me for misbehaving so badly?"

"Of course, don't think a thing about it," I smile, taking the plate and lifting the top. "Mmmm, these look delicious. I have a pot of coffee on...would you like a cup?"

"Oh, that would be lovely, thank you."

"Please, have a seat. I'll be right back." I put the cookies on the table in front of my sofa and go into the kitchen. I pour two mugs and bring them out on a tray with cream, sugar and two spoons. Janet is slowly walking around my apartment, looking at photos on the wall, still clutching her bag. *This isn't going to be easy,* I think. "Here we go," I say a little too brightly as I set the tray on the coffee table.

"Oh, my, is this you with President Obama?" Janet asks.

"Yes, he visited Phoenix a few years ago. I was still in college, but got to cover his trip. Um, may I hang your purse on my coat rack?"

Janet smiles and sits on the sofa, placing her purse close beside her feet. "Oh, no, this is fine, thanks."

"Your hair, you've cut it since Wednesday." I hand a cup to Janet.

Janet's hand flutters to her forehead to adjust the remaining locks.

"Oh, uh, my bangs were getting too long, and I couldn't wait for my next hair appointment."

A likely story. "You know, when I saw you at O'Toole's, it looked like your hair had been singed somehow. Cookie?" I hold out the plate, looking a little more closely at the uneven trim. Janet holds her palm out in refusal.

"No, thanks, they're all for you. Maybe...you saw my hair...frizzy. Yes, that must've been it. It was a bit humid the other day. Now, what kind of a story would you like to do on me?"

"Well, I'd like to find out a little about your background, and about the various groups you work with." I prepare my recorder and put it in front of Janet, who preens as if she were doing a tele-vision interview, putting on lipstick and fluffing her hair.

"Your nails are beautiful, Janet," I remark. "Do you do them yourself or go to a salon?"

"Oh, I don't have the patience. I go to Salon Chic in Scotts-dale."

I make a mental note of the name.

"So, tell me about where you grew up, where you went to col-lege, that sort of thing."

I watch as Janet puts the lipstick and mirror back in her purse, on the floor.

"Oh, I grew up in a little bitty town south of the Valley called Morenci. It's a mining town, you know, but I couldn't wait to leave. There was just nothing to offer a young girl such as myself, and I had so many things I wanted to do.

"So, I moved to Phoenix, went to ASU and joined a sorority. Oh my, did I have a great time! That's really where my love for community service was born, and I have been so fortunate to work with many wonderful organizations and the people in them." She flashes a large smile at me.

"I understand you volunteered on a number of the same com-mittees that Rosemary Thornton did, is that right?"

A dark look briefly enters Janet's eyes, and disappears. "Why, I thought this story was about me, not Rosemary, bless her soul."

"Oh, of course, I'm just trying to establish your involvement in the Cultural Commission, and, let's see, you have been named in-terim president of the Sisters Domestic Violence Shelter, succeeding Rosemary, is that right?"

"Actually, I was on the board, and I volunteered to take over in this time of...well, under circumstances such as these."

"So, what do you suppose happened to Rosemary?" I ask innocently. Janet blinks a few times, and her face reflects surprise at the question.

"Why, she died in that fire, like the news says. I don't know anything else about it, except that it was a very tragic accident. Now, about the Cultural Comm—"

"You must've known Rosemary pretty well, with all the organizations you both belonged to. What was she like?"

Janet's sweet smile looks forced. "Why, she was certainly a strong leader, and a very powerful person who usually got exactly what she wanted. I, on the other hand, prefer—"

I pull out a picture printed from the Internet. *Time to go for it.*

"And you said you only knew her husband 'in passing,'" I interrupt, "yet here's a photo of the three of you at one of the galas. You're standing next to Tyler Jameson and you look quite chummy. And I'm pretty sure you were saying 'Ty' the other day, not 'guy.' Weren't you talking with Tyler at the funeral today?"

Janet sits up straight, that dark look returning, staying this time. "I don't know what you're trying to pull here, but I came on the best of intentions, and I don't like your insinuations."

"I'm sorry, I'm not insinuating anything, I'm just trying to learn more about you."

"Well, it doesn't sound that way." Janet stands up, grabbing her purse. "This interview is over."

"Wait, Janet, I—"

"Enjoy the cookies."

Janet leaves, slamming the door behind her.

"Guess you're not interested in baby kitties, either," I say to the door.

I pick up the beverage items from the table, and look at the cookies more closely. I sniff them, but don't detect anything out of the ordinary. I take everything into the kitchen, where I place all the cookies in a large baggie and zip them up tight.

It's mid afternoon, and I pace in my front room for a few minutes. I'm going a little stir crazy. The kitties are fed, and they're sleeping soundly.

I pick up my phone, press a few buttons and put it to my ear.

"Hi, Detective Ware, this is Lisa again from the radio station...you said I could call you back. Is this a good time to talk?"

I listen for a moment.

"Of course, the offer of a drink still stands," I say. "Uh, but I...um...am having some car challenges. Any chance you could swing by and pick me up?"

I smile with the response.

"Great, tell you what, just meet me at Circle K on the corner of Frye and Arizona Ave…"

I slip out the back of my apartment building and hurry on foot to the convenience food store. *Hey, I'll be with a former cop, so I'll be safe, right?*

A tan older-model Taurus pulls into the store's parking lot, and I barely recognize George Ware from his official police department photo of 20 years ago. I wave at him, and climb in the passenger seat.

"Thanks for meeting me...whoa!" The strong smell of alcohol hits me as I enter the vehicle. George, now in his 60s and quite overweight, sits at the wheel. Perspiration drips down his red face. The few strands of hair sprouting on top of his balding pate are plastered on his forehead.

"Get in, li'l lady," he slurs. He starts to drive off.

"Uh, I'd be happy to drive if you want," I offer, but George waves me off with a pudgy hand.

"Nuthin' wrong with me," he says defiantly, as we pull into traffic. "Just like I had nuthin' to do with bungling that money pickup."

George continues to drive south on Arizona Avenue, passing what's left of Chandler's farm fields, now sprouting thousands of residential homes and condos.

"What...happened that day?" I ask nervously, my eyes watching the street.

"Me 'n' my partner were doin' surveillance where the undercovers planted the bank's dough. It was in a trash can on Grover Street, right underneath a street lamp, easy to see anyone who came by."

He veers off the side of the street as he remembers that day.

"Watch the road, George!"

He swerves back into the center of the lane.

"Then what?" I ask.

"See, thing was, we had already been waitin' there more than 24 hours after the time the ransom note said. We was drinking plenty of coffee to stay awake, but I hadda take a leak bad."

George's eyes were staring straight ahead, his chunky hands gripping the steering wheel, but in his mind, it was 1985 once again.

"I tell my partner, 'Stay on it,' and I get outta the car for a minute. Wasn't no more than that, to do my business, ya know...when I hear a pop. Ya know, the quiet kind that comes from a silencer. I race back around and find Bobby..." His lips tremble, and his glassy brown eyes fill with tears. "He's got a single GSW in his forehead...and the money is gone. Bobby woulda still been here if I hadn't..."

"I'm sorry, George. But it wasn't your fault."

"I know that, but others...Between the whispers, dirty looks, I knew what they was thinkin'..." he trails off.

"That it was an inside job?" I ponder that question while George guns the accelerator and heads further out of town. We're almost at the city limits, and there are fewer houses and mostly brown desert with scrub brush on each side of the roadway. The Gila River Indian Community reservation land is just up ahead.

"Look out!" The Taurus veers over the centerline, with a car coming straight towards us. George turns the wheel to the right with a jerk, going off the pavement into the dirt, and has to turn left again as he overcorrects. The other car's horn blares angrily as it continues in the opposite direction.

"George, look, I think—"

Suddenly, we feel a strong bump from behind us, and I look back to see a black late model vehicle with tinted windows way too close.

"Hey, get the hell off my tail!" George shouts, looking into his rearview mirror. I watch in horror as the car slows down, then speeds up and rams us again, harder this time.

"Oh, shit!" I scream, recognizing the car.

The black vehicle swerves to George's side and sideswipes his car, pushing it off to the right side of the road. I watch as the window of the black car rolls down and a gun comes out.

"George, we gotta get out of here! Floor it!" I cry as George hits the accelerator. A shot rings out, blowing out the back seat window and spraying small pellets of glass everywhere.

"What the hell?" George's expression combines shock, surprise and confusion.

The black vehicle speeds up, races in front of George's car and slams on the brakes.

"George!" I shriek as I grab the wheel and turn it hard to the right. George's car flies into the ditch, comes up the other side and is airborne for a few moments before turning in mid-air. It comes down, hard, on the driver's side, before sliding another fifteen feet in the soft sandy dirt. It finally turns over to rest upside-down.

The black car fishtails down the road, leaving George's in a billow of brown desert dust.

I dream I'm in a circus, on the high wire, swinging upside down from a harness strapped to my tight-fitting attire. I always wondered what it would be like to live a gypsy type of life on the road. My brothers and I loved it when the periodic small circus would come near my hometown. The big tent, the amazing animals, the fantastic costumes, and of course, the cotton candy. I continue to glide, but find it odd that no one cheers or applauds.

As I sway through the air, I wake up. It's not a big top, but I'm still inside George's car. The seat belt straps are holding me snug against the deployed airbags.

I look at George, crumpled on his left side and pinned by the white billowing fabric, but without a seatbelt on. Blood runs down from his forehead, and he's unconscious.

"George...George! Can you hear me?" I call out. No response. Coming out of my daze, I fumble with my car restraint until it releases and I drop onto the car's ceiling.

"Ahhh!" I scream in pain, holding my ribcage. I almost pass out, but manage to ward off the blackness.

"George...you gotta wake up...we have to get outta here..." I crawl slowly, painfully, to the large man, and feel for a pulse.

"Oh, god, no, no, please..." I wail. I shake George, but get no reaction. "Noooo!"

I slide gingerly to the passenger door, and try to open it, but the impact has jammed it. There's no glass in the side window, having been blown out by the earlier gunshot, and I slowly inch my way toward it, body aching and head throbbing from the exertion. I carefully slither out, across the rounded glass pieces, and finally come out on the dry desert floor, full of rocks and dirt and cactus. More agony.

The car is at least a hundred yards from the road, and there are no vehicles in either direction. I slowly pull myself up beside the vehicle, and look around for my bag, spotting it in the back seat. I reach for my cell phone and slowly punch 9-1-1.

A soft "beep-beep" repeats again and again as I try to open my eyes.

I hear a low garbled sound and finally make out two vertical white shapes and another dark one.

"I think she's coming around," one of the white shapes says. "Miss Powers? I'm Dr. Howard, and you are at Chandler Regional Medical Center."

I can't understand why I'm in the hospital, or why even blinking my eyes causes such great pain. The blue shape speaks.

"Lisa, hey, am I glad you're back. You sure scared us there for awhile."

I can't quite make him out, but he sounds familiar. I squint my eyes and wince. I reach my arm up and feel a gauze bandage on my forehead, and see an IV tube snaking out from my left arm.

"Hey, it's Johnstone here, you know, from Chandler PD?"

"Whatcha got working?" I say in a scratchy whisper.

"You. We're workin' you," he says, first with a smile that turns to just a tinge of anger. "Giving my officer the slip...taking off with someone who had no business behind the wheel—"

That gets my attention, and I remember what happened. "George? Is he...?"

"Sorry, kiddo, he didn't make it. His alcohol blood level was off the charts. Add a car wreck to an already burdened heart, and—"

"What about...did you get...the shooter?"

Detective Johnstone glances at the doctor and nurse with a frown, and back to me.

"What...are you talking about?"

"They followed us... same black car...they rammed us...took a shot at us...oh god, it's all my fault..." I close my eyes as they fill with tears. "And the kittens...I gotta feed the kittens..." I try to get up, but pain forces me to sink back into the pillow.

"It's probably just the meds, giving her hallucinations," I hear the doctor tell Johnstone. "I think you'd better go."

"No...happened...wait..." I whisper.

"I...we'll...yeah, okay, but Lisa, you hang in there. It's going to be all right."

The nurse shows Johnstone to the door. My eyes stay open long enough to see his concerned face glancing back at me before he leaves.

Mysterious music fades up full and under, and my voice fills the airwaves.

"Welcome back to 'Murder in the Air Mystery Theatre.' I'm Lauren Price. Tonight on 'Frightful Fun House,' our carnival couple find themselves in the 'Insanitorium' with a human sideshow behind glass

walled rooms—and a real-life dead body. On top of that, Brad disappears."

"Brad, where the hell are you? This better not be some joke!" Spotting a door inside the glass booth, Liz picks up the old woman's cane and starts pounding on the clear walls. "Hey! Someone! Anyone! I need some goddamned help! We need to get out of—"

With that, her last blow with the cane cracks the glass, and shards fly. Liz looks back at the old woman on the floor, gingerly steps across the threshold and opens the door.

Liz steps into a long and narrow hallway, obviously not part of the fun house, with paper cups strewn on the floor, a mop and bucket along one wall and regular lighting hanging from the ceiling.

"Brad? Are you here? Anyone?"

She goes to the end of the hallway, where she nervously puts her hand on the doorknob and slowly turns it. The door opens into a small office with a desk, chair, fake plastic plant—and a small, older man sitting at the table, paper ledgers in front of him, running a calculator. He looks up in surprise. With one hand, he slams shut an open desk drawer.

"Who are you? And how did you get in here?" the man asks.

"Oh, thank god!" Liz cries out. "We were trapped in the Fun House...my boyfriend's missing and there's a dead woman in there! You have to help!"

"Oh my, this is so bizarre," the little man says, jumping to his feet and pacing around his desk. "I...this has never—"

"Call 9-1-1, you idiot!" Liz screams, looking around for a phone. When she doesn't see one, she pulls out her cell to check for service. "Damn! Why can't I get a signal?" she bellows. "And why don't you have a telephone here?"

The little man is shocked.

"We are always on the road...we don't have a telephone line here, only in the main office." He points down the hallway.

Liz takes a breath to calm herself. "And where is that? Would you please take me there?"

The man signals that he'll follow her out the door. But once Liz steps out into the hallway, the man quickly closes the door behind her and turns the lock.

"What the...? Why you little piece of..." Liz turns and bangs on the door. "Open up right now!"

But the door stays closed.

"Nooooo!" Liz yells.

"Why won't the little man help her? How is Liz going to get help, and how can she find Brad? Come back next time for another 'Murder in the Air Mystery Theatre' episode. I'm Lauren Price. Good night."

CHAPTER 7

MONDAY, APRIL 15

I spend a couple of days going in and out of a morphine-induced
sleep. In addition to multiple bumps and bruises, I've fractured
three ribs, which makes breathing painful.

I eventually convince a nurse to retrieve my cell phone. *Shoot.
Three missed calls from Bruce. He'll have to wait.* I dial my landlady.

"Hi, Evelyn, it's Lisa—"

"Oh my goodness, honey, where are you? *How* are you?"

"I'm fine, really...I'm just getting ready...to head for home." I
have difficulty saying more than a few words at a time with the
pain in my lungs and head. "But I have a big favor to—"

"You know, your good friend Mr. Thompson called, and left a
key to your apartment under your doormat."

"He did?"

"And I found everything I needed and am feeding those sweet
little kitties of yours right this minute."

"You are? Oh, that is so great…I really appreciate it…I will be home…later today. How are they doing?"

"Oh, they're so precious, and doing just fine, don't you worry."

I smile. "That's good…to hear…I need to find them…a home…would you…want to keep them?"

"Oh, honey, you know Alfred. I just don't think he'd take to them so well."

I listen, then close my eyes, leaning back into the pillow. "Of course…I understand. Thanks…so much, Evelyn." A tear runs down my face.

There's a knock at my hospital door, which opens far enough to reveal Ron Thompson's worried face.

"Hey, young lady, you up for some company?"

"Sure…come in."

Ron shuffles to my bedside, wearing an anxious expression.

"Ron, where's…your oxygen?" I ask. He's a little gray, and perspiring.

"Oh, I left it in the car. Didn't want anyone thinkin' I belong here," he said smiling.

"Yeah, well, don't stay…too long or they'll…have to find you a bed."

"You gonna be okay?" Ron asks, concerned.

"Of course, don't worry." I try to pull myself up in bed, but the pain stops me. "Owww…"

"Uh, should I get a nurse?"

"No, no, I'm all right...I'll be outta here...very soon. Hey, thanks for helping...with the kitties."

"Ah, no problem. Your landlady's the one doin' all the work. When Johnstone called me about your little escapade, I figured you wouldn't be home anytime soon. Evelyn...sounds like a nice lady." Ron blushes a bit.

"Yes, she is...you'll have to...meet her in person sometime."

There's an awkward pause.

"How's Denise?"

Ron grins. "You certainly do have a one-track mind. She's still pretty shaken up. But you know this probably has little to do with land deals and more to do with drugs."

I nod. "Speaking of which...any word...from the lab?" I ask.

"As a matter of fact, yes." Ron fishes a piece of paper out of his pocket. "First the gloves: what you smelled is $CH3-2CO$, systematically named propanone, also known as acetone. Most commonly used in fingernail polish remover. Does that mean anything to you?"

I digest this information. "It's the same thing...I smelled at Rosemary Thornton's house...after it burnt down. I wonder if it was used...to start the fire. I mentioned 'accelerant' to Lieutenant Rincon...and he gave me...a very strange look...like I wasn't supposed to know...anything about it." I think a moment, and look back at Ron. "And the powder?"

Ron shifts his feet, looking uncomfortable. "It's...potassium cyanide. Very toxic, but can be bought on the Internet. It's found in pesticides, toilet bowl cleaner, even gasoline. But the small amount you gave me for testing? Could kill one person." He pauses. "The whole bag could kill dozens."

"Probably a good thing...I didn't get it back...in Janet's purse." I pause, realizing. "You think...?" I ask.

"It's possible," the older man replies, nodding his head.

I sit, dressed, on the edge of my hospital bed, waiting for my final discharge papers. Evelyn brought me a fresh change of clothes, considering my shirt and pants were torn and bloody from the accident. The speakerphone on my cell is on.

"...And college sports fans, we've got our Final Four. It will be Louisville, in their second straight appearance; Wichita State, in the NC-Double-A championship for their second time ever; Syracuse, the 2003 national champs; and Michigan, returning for the third time. More later in this hour. News is next."

There's a very brief pause before the deep voice of the daytime news anchor takes over.

"Thanks for listening to KWLF-FM Radio. It's 4 o'clock, and this is Pat Henderson. Topping the news today: a happy ending for Mark Rogers and his family, the man who was trying to go bird watching with friends, but ended up spending five days in the wreckage of his car when it went over a ravine outside Jerome. And our Lisa Powers helped with the rescue.

"According to the Associated Press, Rogers' son Jerry told NBC News his dad was temporarily blinded by the sun coming up low in the morning sky. Jerry says his father panicked, braked and the car flipped and plunged down the embankment, landing right next to, but fortunately not in, a small creek. After the accident, with multiple broken bones and unable to move, he ate bugs, the inside of cactus and drank water from the stream.

"Rogers said he could hear cars and see their lights on the road above and hoped he'd be found. But as time passed, he resigned himself to the thought that no one would discover him, and even mentally said goodbye to his family.

"Jerry, his sister Joan, along with KWLF reporter Lisa Powers and former radio reporter Ron Thompson retraced what they thought might have been his route and found tire tracks where his car left the roadway. They discovered Mark Rogers below.

"The elder Rogers suffered five broken ribs, a punctured lung, a broken left leg and multiple bruises, cuts and scratches. A Yavapai County Medical Center spokesperson also said Rogers was doing well and in good spirits—just very hungry.

"Yavapai County Sheriff's investigators are working to determine the cause of the accident," the report continues. "They say that particular section of road has always been treacherous with its sharp curves and steep cliffs. YCSO Sgt. Anthony Cabrillo says, quote, 'This is a bad section of road,' unquote, adding it's the fifth accident they've had with cars over the side. That includes 83-year-old Henry Jacobson, whose body was found next to Jerry Rogers' car. He apparently went over the embankment three weeks earlier.

"Also making news today..."

I turn off the radio app on my phone. A text message "dings." It's Bruce with a short "what the h is going on? U ok?" *I can't deal with him right now.* I punch back "i m fine. will talk later." I call up another number and press a button to dial.

"Joan? It's...Lisa. Sounds like your dad...is doing better?"

"Yes, he's still in the hospital, but it's been a flurry of activity. All these media people calling and wanting interviews. But you're the one who really helped when no one else would. Hey, what's this about your being in an accident? Are you okay?"

"Oh, sure...I'm fine...just a few bruises. Hey, Joan, would you...email me your contact for that...Find Me group? I'd...like to do...a story on them. Include how...the psychic helped."

"I would be more than happy to. They were amazing, and so supportive. I'll send that right off."

A male tech dressed in blue scrubs enters, pushing a wheelchair. "Ready to go?"

I put my hand over the phone.

"Just one sec, please," I say, pointing to the phone.

"Sorry, Joan, my...ride is here. By the way...we found a couple of...newborn kittens outside the station. They're adorable...any chance you would like them?"

"Gosh, I'd love to, but we have three big dogs. But I'll ask around and let you know."

"That would...be great, thanks."

I end the call. "Let's do it," I say as the tech helps me into the wheelchair. "Hey, you like cats?"

Keys in hand, I walk gingerly up to my apartment with Ron at my elbow, but stop when I see the door is open about an inch.

Ron, close behind me, puts a finger to his lips for me to be quiet, and leans his ear toward the door. From inside, he hears a voice.

"Aren't you just the cutest little things in the world?" My landlady, Evelyn, is talking baby talk to the kittens. Relief floods through me, and, as we enter, I see it on Ron's face, too.

"Hello? Evelyn?" I call out.

"Oh, you're home, honey, I'm so glad. Yes, I was just giving these babies their feeding."

She straightens herself up the table where the kittens are curled up in the basket. Smiling, she looks at Ron, who stands stiffly, staring back.

"Evelyn, I'd like you to meet...my good friend, Ron Thompson," I interject. "Ron, this is my...wonderful landlady, Evelyn Jones."

Evelyn reaches out her hand, and a mute Ron shakes it. "It's a pleasure to finally meet you, Mr. Thompson. You know how it is when you only talk to someone by phone. Funny, you're much taller than I imagined." She giggles, a little embarrassed.

Ron finally finds his voice. "Call me Ron. And you're...just as pretty as I imagined." His face turns a deep red.

Evelyn giggles again, and suddenly turns to me. "Oh, honey, you probably need to sit down. Can I get you anything?" She carefully ushers me to the sofa.

"No, really, I'm fine. I'm just so grateful...you could feed the kitties."

"Oh, I was happy to. But I just don't think Alfred—" she looks at Ron—"he's my African Grey parrot—would be too thrilled about sharing our place. But if you ever need any help with them at all, you just let me know. They should be good for another three to four hours."

Evelyn picks up her purse and heads for the door. "Okay, I'll be home if you need anything."

"Thanks again, Evelyn."

"You're welcome." She turns to Ron. "Nice to meet you...Ron. Hope to see you again." She bustles out the door, closing it behind her.

"I think she likes you, Ron," I tease.

"Oh, I'm too old to...you know..."

"What? Too old for conversation? Too old to have dinner? I don't think so. You gotta get out more."

"Yeah, you should talk. Miss Never Dates Anyone, She Who Hangs Out With Old Grumpy Guys. Look, since you gave that assistant D.A. the boot, you tell that sports guy, Bruce, that you'll go out with him, and I'll...well, I will..."

"Yes, you'll what?"

"I'll invite Evelyn for...coffee."

I smile. I think wistfully for a moment about Nate Rickford, the attorney I broke up with last year on Valentine's Day, of all times. "Well, that's a start. Okay, I'll...think about it. Meanwhile, you want a couple of kittens to keep you company?"

The familiar mystery theatre theme song is played, along with my voice.

"The Frightful Fun House is becoming a house of horrors for Liz, when she can't find her boyfriend and the little man she discovers in an office won't call for aid."

Liz runs down the hallway. "Where is everyone?! Why won't anyone help—"

Just then, a door opens at the end of the long hallway. A woman wearing a white coat, carrying a clipboard, steps out. Liz runs to meet her.

"Oh, thank god, you've got to help me! I can't find my boyfriend, and there's a dead body in the Insanitorium!"

"That's impossible, young lady," *the woman says.* "How on earth did you get out here?"

"Through that door...right... I mean...down there..." *Liz turns, pointing down the hall, in different directions, not sure herself. All she sees are long solid walls.*

"There are no doors there, dear," *the woman says gently.*

"But there was...the old lady...she was in the freak sideshow room...and there was a little man in an office at the other end of the hall, but he wouldn't..." *When she looks down the hall, there is only a wall at the end.*

"Now, dear, why don't you come with me and we'll sort this all out." *The woman leads Liz back through the door. They go into what looks like a doctor's office. A tall man with a shock of white hair, also wearing a long white coat, stands.*

"Doctor, this woman appears to be lost," *says the woman.*

"No, I'm...well, I don't know where I am, but it's my boyfriend who's lost, and we were...I saw horrible things..." *Liz collapses, crying.*

"There, there, my dear," soothes the doctor. *"Everything will be all right."*

"Have a drink of water, Miss...?" the woman asks, handing her a glass with clear liquid.

"It's...Liz...I don't know what's going on...Brad, where are you?!" My voice returns.

"Has Liz stumbled into the Frightful Fun House's twilight zone? Things just aren't what they should be...or are they? Find out next time on 'Murder in the Air Mystery Theatre.' I'm Lauren Price. Thanks for joining us."

CHAPTER 8

TUESDAY, APRIL 16

I ease slowly into the rental car, my ribs still causing sharp pain with certain movements.

I drive to the station, taking a moment to look for the mother calico. No sign. The food bowls are turned over and empty, but I assume it could be any number of critters that helped themselves over the past few days.

The newsroom secretary is the first to see me, and rushes over. "Oh, I'm so glad you're okay!" Sally gushes. "Can I get you anything? A cup of coffee?"

"You don't have to," I say, putting my bag by my cubby.

"I'm happy to, you just sit down and I'll be right back."

Pat Henderson waves at me from the control room, and David comes over, a solemn look on his face.

"Glad you're back," he says. "But just a heads-up: Grant is on the warpath."

"Oh. Thanks."

I don't see Grant in the newsroom, so I turn my attention to the pile of mail and phone messages. A number of callers wishing me well, a few others from people with story ideas for me. I power up my computer, and glance over the dozens of emails I'll need to go through. But I open one from Detective Johnstone.

Call me. Got an update. Joe.

I anxiously pick up the phone and dial, as Sally brings me a mug of coffee. Smiling my thanks, Johnstone's voice picks up on the other end.

"Hi, Joe, it's Lisa. Whatcha got working?"

"You may not remember me visiting you in the hospital, but—"

"Of course I do. I appreciate your coming."

"You said something that I thought was kinda strange at the time…"

"About another shooter? No, it wasn't the meds…although they did give me some strange dreams. Did you find something?"

"Well, we were just investigating it as a vehicular accident, and everything seemed consistent with that. You know, the car was pretty beat up."

"Yeah, and?"

"And, well, when you said something about being rammed, and getting shot at, we looked again. Sure enough, not only did we see back bumper damage, but we also found a slug behind the front seat."

"Let me guess: same calibre as at Denise's house."

"You got it."

There's a pause as this sinks in. Out of the corner of my eye, I see Grant come in the newsroom from the front entrance with a grim look on his face. He's coming toward me.

"So, Lisa, that means…"

Grant is standing in front of me.

"Uh, Joe, I have a bunch of questions, but I'm going to have to call you back."

I hang up and swivel my chair toward Grant. "Hey, I'm fine, the accident just looked a lot worse than…"

"Conference room. Now." Grant turns on his heels and leaves.

I gulp. I glance at David, who is cleaning some equipment. He raises his eyebrows in an "I told you" manner and goes back to his work.

I steel myself with a swig of coffee and follow Grant.

"Good morning, Lisa." Station Manager Terry Tompkins' deep voice booms from where he's sitting at the large, shiny conference table in a room that still smells faintly of leather and wood polish. A long-time broadcast executive, he started in the business as a radio announcer and moved up the ranks. He's been running the station for the past five or more years, and is generally known to be fair in most dealings with employees. "Please have a seat." Grant takes the seat next to him, hands clenched together tightly, looking very angry.

"Good morning, sir," I say meekly, sinking into a large leather chair. "Look, I can explain—"

"No, you look," Grant interrupts, the veins on his neck and forehead bulging. "You have put yourself and others in danger—"

"Me?! Hey, I didn't know I was gonna get shot at," I counter.

"You should never have gotten into that car with that drunk—" Grant starts.

"Now, just calm down, you two." Tompkins soothing voice settles the air. "What Grant means to say is we're concerned about you, Lisa, and that this story has gotten out of control. We want you to hold off and let the police do their job."

"But we're close to solving—"

"The police solve the crimes, we just report on them." Grant is livid. "You have been reckless with some of your decisions of late, and we have...liabilities." He pauses for a moment, softening. "I know you're young, and you're eager. Those are admirable qualities for a journalist." The veins bulge again, and he clenches his jaw. "But we report the news, we don't make the news." He pauses for a beat. "You are on administrative leave with pay until further notice. Take your things and head home."

"Wait, what?!"

"It's for your own safety, Lisa," Tompkins adds gently.

"Fine." I get up too fast, and close my eyes against the blackness that almost overtakes me. "You know how to reach me." I am seething, but don't want them to know it. I rush back into the newsroom, hiding the discomfort the soreness causes, past several sets of silent eyes watching my every step, grab my bag, stuff my mail inside and without saying a word, exit out the back door.

Once outside, the tears of anger and embarrassment fill my eyes as I fumble for my car keys.

I sob as I call Ron from inside my car.

"Ron, I can't believe what they've done!" I cry. "What am I going to do?"

"Hold on, young lady, slow down. What are you talking about?"

"I'm on 'administrative leave with pay.' And they sent me home!"

Ron pauses. "Grant did that?"

"Grant and Tompkins. For making 'reckless decisions,' they said. 'It's for your own safety,'" I say facetiously. "What the hell does it mean, anyway?"

"Hey, not to worry. Happens all the time. The fact that they're still paying you is good. Probably means they want things to cool down a little. And I would agree: they probably want to protect you from any further harm."

I sniff, and reach for a tissue. "So what, I don't work 'until further notice?' I don't go into the station? I don't write stories? I just sit in my apartment? I'll go crazy!"

"Well, we could bang out a few extra podcasts," Ron offers. I don't respond. "Look, so you don't physically go to the station. Did they say anything about not making phone calls?"

I think for a moment. "No, they really didn't say anything else. I was upset, so I grabbed my stuff and left." I blow my nose. "So, hey, I can use my own personal cell phone any way I want, right?" I'm feeling more confident. "I can still talk to people, and keep working the stories from home. They'll never know!"

"Now, don't get carried away. It will probably do you good to relax for a few days, get your body healed. This will all blow over, and you'll be back before you know it."

"I hope you're right, Ron." I take a big breath. "Guess I'll be spending some quality time with those kittens."

"Speaking of which, have you named 'em yet?"

"Nah, I can't keep 'em, and the new owner should do that. I gotta find someone who can give them lots of attention, pick their names, all that."

"I don't know, you'd be surprised how easy cats are to take care of, not like dogs. But whatever you think is best. You okay now?"

"Yeah, I'm better, thanks a lot. Sorry for losing it like that."

"You've been there for me. It's the least I can do."

I start my rental car. "Ya know, maybe you're right. I can spend some time on the podcast script, and we'll record a few ahead."

"Atta girl. Now, you go straight home and lock your door."

"Yes, sir!" I smile. "Talk to you later."

So maybe this administrative leave won't be so bad, I think. *Don't know how I'm going to explain this to everyone, but...*I stop that thought when I see a dark vehicle following not far behind me. *Oh crap, don't tell me!* I turn right at the next corner, and the car turns as well. *If I go home, they'll know where I live. Who are you fooling? They probably know where you live already. Maybe I should go back to the station. No. Maybe to the police department—yeah, that's it, I'll call Johnstone and have him meet me outside.*

I speed dial the detective, who takes four rings to answer. I get more impatient.

"Joe! I've got someone following me, what should I do?!"

"What's your 20?"

"Um, I'm coming up to the corner of Alma School and Queen Creek. It's a dark car, but I can't tell if it's the same..."

"Hold on."

I hear Joe say something on a walkie-talkie in the background. He starts chuckling.

"What the hell are you laughing at, Joe, this is not funny!"

"No, you're right, it's not. Okay, so pull off to the side of the street, like you're parking."

I pull to the right and stop in a white-lined spot.

"What's the car doing?"

"Oh, shit, he's right behind me, Joe! Now what?" I shriek.

"Does the driver have on a striped polo shirt and a baseball cap?"

"Huh?"

I peer into me rear-view mirror.

"Oh, yeah, I think so."

"And can you see if the vehicle is a Crown Vic?"

"That's a Ford, right?"

"Right. And is the driver waving a badge at you?"

"Shit, Joe, he's with you? Why didn't someone tell me? And I thought you were so short-staffed?"

"Turns out someone high up in your food chain talked to someone high up in my food chain...and suddenly we have you covered 24/7."

"No kidding?"

"No kidding, Lisa. Now just go straight home and don't break any traffic laws or Harry will have to arrest you."

"Very funny." I turn to look back at the officer behind me, and wave. Harry smiles, raising his forefinger in my direction as an acknowledgement.

"Thanks, Joe," I say sheepishly. "So, can I call you later and get an update?"

"Actually, here's what I need you to do: Let Harry go in your apartment first and check it out. Then he's going to take a report on the whole George Ware incident. Tell him everything you remember about the other car, and call me when you're done. Harry will be on security outside your place for the rest of the shift, and at three we'll send another car."

"Jeez, Joe, is this really necessary?"

"Obviously a number of people think so."

Harry Dugan, a big bear of a man with an easy smile, goes to my door ahead of me. But now he's all business, and with Glock drawn, indicates for me to unlock the entrance. He pushes open the door, the sight of the gun following his eyes as he surveys the room.

"Stay here," he says, pointing to just inside the entryway, and closes the front door. He goes into the kitchen, down the hall into the bathroom and my bedroom before returning to me, holstering his gun. He smiles and sneezes, a big "wah-CHOO" exploding from his body.

"'Scuse me," he says, pulling out a handkerchief from his back pocket and wiping his nose. "All clear." But he turns sharply as he hears a noise behind him, whipping his weapon out again. "What's that?" I walk around him, reach down and pick up the basket holding two tiny bundles of fur stirring and wanting to be fed.

"Ah, ain't those the tiniest li'l things you ever saw?" Harry puts his firearm away again, and reaches over to gently stroke one kitten. "Wah-CHOO!" he sneezes again. "May I?" he asks. I hand one to Harry, who gently cuddles it in his large hands.

"Harry, I think you need a couple of kittens to take home," I say encouragingly. "I'll give you plenty of food, their kitty litter box and I'll even throw in a cat carrier."

"Yeah, they sure are cute, but sorry, I'm allergic to 'em," he replies. "But I'll ask around in the precinct. Now, I gotta take your statement." He hands the little one back to me, and I put them both in their bed.

"Make yourself comfortable, Harry, and let me get these little guys some food. Would you like something to drink?"

"Water would be swell, if it's no trouble."

"Not at all."

Harry looks out the windows and pulls my blinds shut, and locks the front door before taking a seat on the sofa. He takes out a small notebook and pen from his front shirt pocket, and flips a few pages.

"So, you married, Harry?" I ask as I prepare the eyedropper with the special milk for the kittens.

"Divorced. Live alone now. After a crazy day on the job, I like the peace 'n quiet."

"I know what you mean. Newsrooms are noisy, busy places, too."

Harry watches me with the little ones. "You sure seem to know a lot about cats."

"Oh, well, I grew up with a bunch of them on our farm. Never took care of ones this small, though. Good thing is, what I don't know I can find on the Internet." I chuckle as I squeeze a little milk into the open mouths of the kittens. "But you're gonna be just fine, aren't you?" I murmur to the animals.

Harry asks lots of questions about the shooter, the driver, the gun, how many times they rammed them, George Ware and on and on.

Finally, when he can think of nothing else to ask, the officer bids me goodbye, saying he would be outside in his car until about 3 p.m., when the next shift officer would replace him. He tells me if anything out of the ordinary happens—anything at all —I am to call 9-1-1. If I need to go anywhere, an officer will escort me to my car and wherever I go. He also gives me his card with his number and email on it, and tells me he'll be in touch about the kittens if he has any luck finding a home for them.

Now, I'm used to leaving early and coming home late, so it feels really odd being at the apartment in the middle of the day. At first, I walk around, just checking things out, stopping occasionally to look outside at Harry's car. Finally I go to my computer and type in "what is administrative leave."

One answer that comes back says: "Placing an employee on administrative leave for investigative purposes is not a disciplinary action and cannot itself be used as proof of wrongdoing. It should not harm an employee's record or affect his performance evaluation."

Hmmm. That doesn't sound so bad. And if they're really willing to pay for extra security, well, maybe they're not so awful after all.

I pull the story files from my bag and put them on my small computer desk, along with my cell phone. I stare at them for a moment, then get up and head to the kitchen. I survey the contents of the refrigerator: miscellaneous to-go boxes, diet Coke, regular Mountain Dew and some butter. *Never made it to the store.* I decide to treat myself to the Dew, and pour it over some ice, taking it back to my office area. I call Detective Johnstone.

"Joe, it's Lisa. Got any more info on that gun?"

He takes a beat. "Uh, I thought you were on A.L."

"Huh?"

"Administrative leave. When it's a police officer, like in the case of a shooting, it means a few automatic vacation days. No working on cases."

"What?! They just told me I was on leave with pay and to go home. They didn't say anything about that."

"Just saying, that's usually what it means."

"Look, Joe, I'll go crazy just sitting around here all day. I've got too many stories I'm working on!"

"So, lay off the cold case for now. That's become way too hot at the moment, pardon the pun."

"Fine." My brain shifts gears. "Okay, how about the Thornton house fire? Anyone found an accelerant?"

Joe pauses a moment. "What do you know about that?" he asks carefully.

"Um, nothing really, I just asked Rincon at Fire the same thing, and he had the identical reaction. So, was something found?"

I hear Joe blow out a deep breath. "This is strictly off the record, kiddo, and I mean it. We'll probably have an official comment in a day or so, but an arson team is being formed and will investigate. If you know anything about it..."

"Hey, I just have my reporter suspicions, that's all. When I was at the scene the day after, I smelled something oddly sweet, like fingernail polish remover. You might mention that to your team."

"Hmm, yeah, I will. Anything else?"

I hesitate. *I don't have enough evidence yet, and don't want to get Janet in trouble. For all I know, maybe she was just trying to get rid of a stubborn weed.*

"Lisa?"

"No, nothing else, just checking through my files. I...have a couple of theories, but I don't want to sound incredibly stupid without more information."

"Okay, but you'll come to me if those theories of yours take hold, right?"

"Sure, Joe, you know I will."

I have always worked well with Joe in the past, so I hate keeping things from him. *But if it turns out to be nothing...*except I know my gut instincts are generally pretty good.

I call Salon Chic in Scottsdale and put on my best highbrow accent.

"Hello, this is Susan calling on behalf of the late Rosemary Thornton," I say. "As you may know, Ms. Thornton recently passed away in a tragic fire, and..."

"Oh, we know, we saw it on the news. That is just terrible!" a young woman exclaims on the other end.

"So, I was just calling to make sure you cancelled any future appointments she may have had."

"Right. Let me check the computer. Yep, she was scheduled for a manicure in a week."

"That was part of her standing schedule every...?" My voice trails off for the receptionist to fill in the blank.

"Looks like every two weeks."

Yes! "And, do you happen to have a note in your files as to her favorite shade of polish?"

"Hmmm, let me see. Yes, it's a deep red called 'Color So Hot it Berns'—spelled b-e-r-n-s." She stops. "Oooh, that's freaky."

"Indeed. Thank you, you've been very helpful." I end the call. *So, if she got her nails done every two weeks, what was Rosemary doing with fingernail polish remover in her living room? She probably wasn't. Even if she had chipped a nail, she'd probably go in to have it fixed.*

Having sent Janet's cookies with Ron yesterday to be tested, I consider calling him for an update, but figure it's too soon to get results. The missing dad story is essentially done for another couple of weeks. I know I'll do a follow-up once Mark Rogers is able to talk about his ordeal, but that's a ways off.

I hear rustling from the kitty box, so go to check on them. I pick one up, and realize that its eyes are starting to open. It's so tiny, the kitten fits in one hand with lots of room to spare. "Let's see, I think you're about eight days old now. Are you hungry again, little one?" I glance at the kitchen clock: 12:30. "It's lunch time for all of us, I guess." I feed the kitties and clean them up with a soft cloth. They huddle together and go back to sleep.

I look again in my 'fridge, peer in one of the brown boxes and wrinkle my nose. I pitch it in the trash. I open the other one, but put it back. I open the freezer door to find it mostly covered with snowy-looking ice. The sole item inside is an empty ice cube tray.

Finding Harry's card, I call the number on it.

"Somethin' wrong?" he asks.

"No, I'm fine, thanks. But it's lunchtime, and I thought I'd order a pizza. Wanna join me?"

"Sure, if that's okay. It beats the peanut butter 'n' jelly sandwich I made this morning. But I gotta check out the pizza delivery guy, just in case."

The young, wide-eyed and pimply-faced kid in his early 20s who brings the sausage, mushroom and extra cheese pizza has obviously never been frisked by a police officer, and I give him an healthy tip for the experience.

"So, Harry, what do you know about Chandler's arson squad?" I ask, taking a bite. I subtly watch him for his reaction.

"Not much. I'm just a patrol guy." Harry curls his pizza lengthwise and eats half of it at once. "But usually, one's from fire, one's from P.D., and I think the county attorney's office assigns someone, too. 'Course, they gotta have special training. Why?" He wipes grease off his chin with a napkin.

"Oh, we've been covering that Rosemary Thornton fire, and I hear they may think it's arson," I say casually, taking a sip of soda.

"Yeah, I heard somethin' about that, too. Sounds like the deceased didn't have a whole lotta friends, if you know what I mean."

"Yeah, neighbors told me that, too. So, do they suspect someone?"

"Uh, hold on, I...you gotta talk to the PIO boys. I'll get inta trouble for flappin' my gums."

"It's okay, Harry, I won't say anything."

I clean up the kitchen, and wrap up a couple of remaining pieces of pizza for Harry. After lunch, Harry strokes the kittens again and sneezes before heading back out to his car.

I take a big breath and call Grant.

"Look, Grant, I'm really sorry about everything that's happened. Truly I am. I never thought—"

"Well, that's part of the problem, Lisa," Grant interrupts. "Sometimes you don't think. Hopefully you will spend some time this week reflecting on what you might have—"

"This week?" I interrupt. "Not the whole week, please, I have too many stories to work on. In fact, I just found out that an arson team has been put together on the Thornton fire case, and—"

"What do you mean? Have you still been working? You are on—"

"I know, I know, administrative leave, but with all due respect, Grant, no one really told me exactly what that means."

"It's designed to...we don't typically use it much, so...what did you say about the arson team?"

A little smile turns up the corners of my lips.

"We're not supposed to know about it yet. My theory is someone used acetone from fingernail polish remover to start the fire."

Grant pauses. "Now, look, I'll take that story from here. Administrative leave means no working, and you get paid time off until we—"

"But Grant, don't you think I'd be safer at the station with people around than here all alone in my apartment? Sure, they've got a cop outside on the street, but if the newspaper catches wind of the taxpayer dollars used to provide security for me, well, I think they'd have a field day with it. I promise I won't work on the cold case, just this fire story. Please? Pretty please?" I beg.

"I don't know. I've got to talk to legal. You just stay put, and keep off the phone, and off these cases, at least for the rest of the day. I'll let you know what I find out."

"Okay, thanks, Grant!"

I can live with that, I think. I hang up and start to do a happy dance. But my rib pain causes me to double over and I slump carefully into a kitchen chair to catch my breath.

Maybe I could use a nap.

Music from the mystery theatre theme song plays, followed by my voice as the host, Lauren Price.

"It's another episode of 'Murder in the Air Mystery Theatre.' Our 'Frightful Fun House' heroine, Liz, has apparently reached safety, but there's still no sign of her boyfriend, Brad."

In the distance, sound effects fade in of a hodge-podge of voices and noises, but at first, nothing distinguishable. A carny voice becomes clearer, saying "Step right up," along with wild laughter, screams, carousel music, and Brad's voice calling "Liz, where are you?"

Liz bolts upright, finding herself on a small bed inside the now-silent and plain room. There's a small table with a lamp and her blinking cell phone, and an empty rocking chair across the room.

"Hello? Is anyone there?"

Liz gets up, picks up her phone and walks cautiously to the door. Just as she reaches for the knob, the door opens. On the other side is the man with the white hair, but now he's wearing a regular suit.

Behind him is a smiling Brad.

"Brad! Oh my god, thank goodness you're okay!" she cries, running to him. They fall into each other's arms. "Where did you go? How did you find me?"

"They really got us, huh?" Brad starts, shaking his head in disbelief. "I've heard of optical illusions and special effects in a funhouse, but never one that messes with your head like this one!"

"Wha...I mean, you're saying—" Liz stammers.

"It was all part of the act, part of the fun house!" Brad says grinning. "I'll recommend this place anytime!"

"But...what about the dead woman? The old lady?"

The man in the suit coat smiles at Brad.

"That was just a plant, Liz, she wasn't real," Brad explains.

"But...you felt her...you said she was cold, and she wasn't breathing!" Liz is incredulous.

"Again, good special effects, huh?" Brad says confidently. He turns to the "doctor."

"Thanks for a great show, Mac." Brad pumps Mac's hand enthusiastically. "Come on, Liz, let's go home," he says to a bewildered Liz, leading her out the door. Liz's phone beeps.

"Wait a minute," Liz says, stopping in her tracks. "What about this story on my phone?"

She points the mobile toward Brad, who reads:

"Woman found dead at Frightful Fun House Carnival; Foul play is not ruled out."

"Perhaps the special effects were not that special after all. Tune in next time to learn more about how the woman died—and what part Liz and Brad played in her untimely death—when 'Murder in the Air Mystery Theatre' continues. I'm Lauren Price, good night."

CHAPTER 9

WEDNESDAY, APRIL 17

I rise early, despite having turned my alarm off the night before.

The Vicodin pain pill I took yesterday afternoon knocked me out and made me sleep soundly. Slowly waking up to a typical bright and sunny day, I ease myself out of bed. I stretch cautiously, relieved at feeling only a small twinge of pain in my ribs. I check my cell phone by the bed: no messages.

I gently get up and head to the kitchen. A rustling in the cat basket distracts me, and I peer in. Gazing up at me are the tiny wide eyes of one of the kitties.

"Oh, look at you," I murmur, picking up the ball of fur and holding it up high. The cat's eyes are big and round, a light shade of tan. They seem to be looking at me with hope and anticipation. "Are you hungry?" I say. "I'll bet you are."

I gather the special kitty milk and eyedropper, and both kittens eat a lot for their tiny stomachs. As I am cleaning them, I look to determine their gender: one girl, one boy.

"Maybe I should figure out what to call you two." I think for a moment. "Hmmm, Bonnie and Clyde? Nah, overdone. Lucy and Ricky? Or Karen and Richard, for the Carpenters?" I stroke the little ones gently, pondering appropriate monikers. "Or maybe...Cronkite and Walters for two great TV people. Not sure yet. I still think your new owners would probably rather name you."

I cuddle the other one, whose eyes are almost open, too. "You're gonna be next to see this wacky world, munchkin. I'd keep you both, but I'm gone so much, I just don't think I'd be a very good mom right..."

My cell rings with its Norah Jones "Don't Know Why" tune. I put the kitty down and eagerly grab the phone.

"Hello, this is Lisa," I say, knowing full well it's Grant from his caller ID.

"Grant here," he replies.

"And how are you this morning?" I ask uncharacteristically.

"Uh, I'm fine, I guess. And you? How are you feeling?"

"I am feeling much better, thanks," I say enthusiastically. "Any word from the lawyer?"

"Well, against my better judgment, legal says you can come to the station to work, but only on the fire case, nothing else at the moment. You're still going to have security coming and going from work, and overnight. Got it?"

I glance out the blinds and see Harry's undercover car parked on my street. He's inside, drinking from a travel mug.

"Absolutely, no problem, you won't regret this!"

"Make sure I don't," he says.

I dress for work in my trademark khakis, polo and Crocs. I call my landlady to ask her to feed the kittens at noontime, and head downstairs. My tap on Harry's window startles him.

"Good morning, Harry! It's a great day, isn't it?"

"Hey, you was s'posed to call me before comin' down," Harry says, getting out of his vehicle quickly, and scanning up and down the street.

"Oh, sorry, Harry, I forgot. Guess what: they're letting me work at the station today, isn't that terrific? So you can follow me there, and then you don't have to hang around all day long. This has got to be very boring."

"Let's just say I been on worse surveillance jobs," he says as he walks me to my car, opens the door and helps me inside. "Give me a sec to get back to my vehicle, and I'll follow you in. Don't forget to lock."

I hit the lock button and start the car. I watch as Harry ambles back to his car, and we both pull out together.

There's no sign of the mother calico as I approach the station's back door, and I wave to Harry, who watches me go inside.

When they see me, a couple of people in the newsroom do a fist pump, and Sally applauds silently as I beam from ear to ear. I give them a thumbs up and go straight to my desk. *Oh, it's so good to be here.* I'm powering up my computer when Grant comes over.

"Now, look—" he starts.

"I know, I know. I'll behave, really I will." I pause a moment. "I'm going to call PD and get an update on the arson team and see if they've found anything. Then, if you think it's okay, I'd like to call this Find Me organization that Joan Rogers-Hartley used. A DEA guy who now lives in the Valley started it, and they're now a national group. They have a good track record, and use some unusual search techniques. Might make a good soft feature."

"Glad you're back," he says with a tired smile.

"Thanks. You have no idea…"

I put in a call to Kelly Snyder, the retired Drug Enforcement Administration agent and founder of Find Me. According to the organization's website, since 2002 the group has helped police locate missing people around the world. They use retired law enforcement personnel, search and rescue volunteers with canines, experts in handwriting analysis—and "intuitive consultants," or psychics. Joan Rogers-Hartley sure seemed convinced of their abilities. Seems worthy of a story.

With 25 years of experience, Snyder also volunteers with the National Center for Missing and Exploited Children (NCMEC). He's not in, so I leave a message with the receptionist.

My next call is to Chandler PD and Detective Johnstone, who is rather surprised to hear from me.

"I'm only working the Thornton fire story, but my boss agreed I would probably be safer here than all alone at home. No offfense, " I tell him.

"No offense taken. Helps our budget. What's up?"

"Yesterday you said an arson team was being put together. If that's the case, this story goes in a whole new direction."

Joe sighs. "Yes, we are in the preliminary stages of putting the arson team together, but that does not mean—I repeat, it does *not* mean it is arson. They did find a high concentration of acetone around where the woman died, but they also found a bottle of fingernail polish. So, she may have just been painting her nails and—"

"Do you know the name of the polish?" I interrupt.

"Huh?"

"The specific name of the fingernail polish. Can you read a name?"

"Uh, I'd have to ask Fire. What difference does that make?"

"Maybe a lot."

My desk phone rings, and the caller ID shows Snyder, Kelly. I hurry to pick it up.

"Hello, this is Lisa."

"Hi, this is Kelly Snyder from Find Me, returning your call," a deep voice answers. In my mind, I picture Snyder from his website photo: a shock of white hair and gentle looking face.

"Thanks so much. I recently wrote a series of stories on a local missing man, and the Rogers family says your group helped. May I ask you a few questions about your organization?"

"Of course. Joan said you might contact me."

I press Record on my phone. "Okay, I got the basic information from your website. How many cases has your group been able to solve?"

"Currently there are more than 30 cases we have been involved in to help find a missing person. In some cases, the person was alive, in others, they were not, but at least we helped families find closure."

"In the Rogers' case, how did you help?"

"Well, Joan contacted us, and we dispatched a team consisting of a retired police detective, a psychologist and an intuitive consultant, all who donated their time. They met with the family, and helped them be more proactive in their search."

"Now, this intuitive consultant—that's a psychic, right? And, according to Joan, the psychic said her dad was still alive, but hurt. I know it really helped her stay positive. But why psychics? Why not just use standard police work?"

Snyder chuckles. "Why not psychics? They've been used for years by law enforcement, but you just don't hear about it as much. If a medium can help shed some light on a case, it may provide more information than we had to begin with."

"I see you don't charge for your services. How do you operate?"

"That's right, all of our assistance is given for free. We have various fundraisers throughout the year, and we rely on donations.

We also now have a book called *Find Me* and all the profits go to the organization."

"How much does a search cost?"

"On average, to transport equipment and volunteers it can be anywhere from $1,500 to $15,000. With our recent high-profile cases, our call-out requests have increased, but our funds have been depleted. It's heartbreaking to be unable to help each and every family who needs us."

"I understand. Anything else you'd like to add?"

"We are a dedicated group made up of retired law enforcement, about one hundred vetted intuitive consultants from all around the world, and canine search-and-rescue professionals. We are proud of our work and of our members."

"And your office is right here in Chandler?"

"Correct, off Riggs Road."

"We'll also include your website for more information. That's find me, the number two, dot com, right?"

"Right, thanks, Lisa."

"Thank you, Mr. Snyder. And good luck to you."

While it's still fresh in my mind, I turn to my computer and write:

ANNOUNCER LEAD-IN:
The recent disappearance of 67-year-old Mark Rogers of Chandler got local police involved along with a group called "Find Me," dedicated to locating missing children and adults. Lisa Powers has more on this organization that also uses intuitive consultants, or psychics, to help solve cases.

LISA POWERS VOICEOVER:

When Mark Rogers went missing on his way to a bird-watching trip with friends, his family was frantic. They didn't suspect foul play, but neither did they believe the retired Intel engineer would simply leave his wife of 48 years and his two adult children.

JOAN ROGERS-HARTLEY SOUNDBITE:

"He's always been a good father, a loving husband. He wouldn't just leave without saying something."

LISA POWERS VOICEOVER:

When police didn't react as quickly as the Rogers family hoped, they turned to a nonprofit organization based in Arizona called "Find Me." It was created by Kelly Snyder, a former DEA agent who spent time with the National Center for Missing and Exploited Children. He formed the group when he decided he wanted to help locate kids and adults who had disappeared.

I rewind the audio recording to find the quote, marking the spot, and key it into the computer.

KELLY SNYDER SOUNDBITE:

"We are a dedicated group made up of retired law enforcement, about one hundred vetted intuitive consultants from all around the world, and canine search-and-rescue professionals. We are proud of our work and of our members."

LISA POWERS VOICEOVER:

The "intuitive consultants" Snyder refers to are various types of psychic mediums, who also volunteer their time to help find missing persons. These individuals use various abilities such as clairvoyance, or the supernatural power of seeing objects or actions; clairaudience, or a psychic hearing ability; clairsentience, the ability to feel the physical and emotional states of others; spiritualism, or speaking with spirits; and more.

I listen to the audio again and find another soundbite I want to use.

KELLY SNYDER SOUNDBITE:
"Why not psychics? They've been used for years by law enforcement, but you just don't hear about them as much. If a medium can help shed some light on a case, it may provide more information than we had to begin with."

LISA POWERS VOICEOVER:
A psychic told Joan Rogers-Hartley she believed her dad was, quote, "alive but hurt," unquote. He was found injured about a week later, the victim of a car accident.

The outcome wasn't as positive in the case of Jesus Vasquez, a young Tempe man who disappeared after partying near Arizona State University last year. But according to Snyder, Find Me psychics pinpointed a location and its law enforcement personnel with four K-9 units traveled to the scene. Following the Find Me information, officials drained Tempe Lake, and Tempe Fire Department's dive team located Jesus' body 30 feet from the predicted location.

Find Me's services are free, but it costs the group up to $15,000 to send out volunteers and transport equipment. With more high-profile cases, the requests are straining their budget.

KELLY SNYDER SOUNDBITE:
"It's heartbreaking to be unable to help each and every family who needs us."

LISA POWERS VOICEOVER:
Donations may be made at findme number 2 dot com; that's findme2.com, or at KWLF.com, which also has a link to their website. For KWLF Radio, this is Lisa Powers.

I look over the story again, and print a couple of copies. I label the digital tape and leave it with the scripts.

Back on the Internet page with Rosemary's photos, I locate the woman who spoke at the funeral Saturday. The tall, elegant woman with the Chandler Food Bank is Lillian Banks, and I find a phone number for her and call.

"Hello, Mrs. Banks?" I say when a woman answers.

"Yes?"

"I'm Lisa with KWLF Radio, and I heard you speak very eloquently at Rosemary Thornton's funeral Saturday. Is Janet Fradley also involved in your organization?"

"Yes, Janet is on a subcommittee, why?"

"I was just curious. Janet doesn't seem to be in the same, shall we say, financial standing as Rosemary. How did she get in the group?"

"We don't discriminate based on annual incomes, dear. Anyone who is willing to volunteer their time is welcome to help. Perhaps you'd be interested—"

"Uh, you know, the way I could best help is to do a story about your cause, which I would be happy to do. Did you ever note any jealousy between Janet and Rosemary?"

"I don't feel comfortable talking about—"

"So there was some friction?" I interject.

"Dear, we receive donations of food and cash for the needy. We don't have time for such nonsense. Let me know if I can be of further assistance." Mrs. Banks hangs up.

I lean back in my chair and look around the newsroom. An on-air anchor is busy in the studio. Grant is on the phone, and I know he can't see my computer screen anyway. I Google "heroin addiction" and find DrugFreeAZ.org. I discover that heroin is a "highly addictive drug derived from morphine, which is obtained from the opium poppy. It is a 'downer' or depressant that affects the brain's pleasure systems and interferes with the brain's ability to perceive pain."

I see photos of the drug, showing heaps of powder ranging in color from white to dark brown, and even a tar-like substance.

I read on: "Heroin can be used in a variety of ways, depending on user preference and the purity of the drug. Heroin can be injected into a vein, called mainlining; injected into a muscle; smoked in a water pipe or standard pipe; mixed in a marijuana joint or regular cigarette; and burned on aluminum foil. Users can inhale the smoke through a straw, known as 'chasing the dragon,' or snort the powder via the nose."

I start to read about short and long-term effects, but Grant ends his call and I click the screen back over to my calendar.

I head to the kitchen for a break.

Digging coins out of my pocket for the beverage machine, I select a Mountain Dew, which comes thumping down into the bottom tray. I cautiously bend down, holding my side, and retrieve the beverage. It fizzes after I twist off the top, and I take a sip, thinking.

Sally sticks her head in the door. "I'm ordering Chinese for lunch. Want something?"

"Sure, thanks, my usual, please," I reply as Sally disappears. I pull out my cell phone and speed dial Ron.

"Hey, Ron, I'm working on that fire story, and—"

"Hold on, young lady. I thought you were on leave?"

"Oh yeah, jeez, I haven't talked to you since yesterday morning. Well, the leave lasted about a day and a half, which included 24/7 security, then I convinced Grant I'd be safer here at work than by myself in the apartment. I'm only working on the fire story, and I'm waiting on the name of the fingernail polish found in Rosemary's house, but I'm running into dead ends trying to link Janet Fradley with anything. Oh, and the kittens' eyes are opening!"

There's a long silence. "Ron, you there? You okay?"

"I need a nap after hearing all of that," he chuckles.

"Don't s'pose there's any word back about the cookies?"

"No way. My buddy said maybe at the end of the week, which means it also might not be 'til Monday. How are you feeling?"

"Oh, much better, thanks. I'm still a little sore here and there, but I'm glad to be back at work. Oh, I almost forgot about this: I heard Janet Fradley having words with Tyler Jameson at his wife's funeral. So, how do I find a connection between the two?"

"Not so fast, I'm trying to keep up. What did you say about the polish?"

"Well, I called the Salon Chic in Scottsdale, and they gave me the name of the red polish that Rosemary always wore. They said she had a standing appointment every two weeks to get her nails done, so there wouldn't be much reason for her to be doing her nails at home. PD says they found a bottle of polish, and I've asked Joe to check the name of it." I pause. "What if Janet drugged and killed Rosemary with the cyanide, planted the polish and spread polish remover around to start the fire wearing those latex gloves she threw away at her house?"

"Whoa, wait a minute. That's a helluva story."

"I know, I know. But you think it's possible?"

Ron doesn't answer that question. "What about this Jameson guy? Find anything on him?"

"Not much. Only Google hit was the society page when he and Rosemary got married. I tried to talk to him a couple of times, but he wants nothing to do with the media. Called us a bunch of vultures."

"Present company excluded, you know he isn't far off."

"True. So what next? I'm open for suggestions."

"Do a public records search through the county assessor's offiffice. It might show any personal property he owns. You can also check with Superior Court and see if he's ever been through the system. Did you say he liked to fish? Might check Fish & Game for licenses."

"Great stuff."

"Let me see if my private investigator friend can run his name through PACER and DMV, see what comes up."

"Thanks, Ron, you're the best!"

I search the assessor's office website for Jameson, but come up with nothing. There are a number of properties owned by Rosemary Thornton, including the mansion that burned, plus a house on Coronado and one in Durango. Maricopa County Superior Court is the same: no civil or criminal cases in his name.

On the AZ Fish & Game website, there's only a place to apply for a license. I pick up the phone and dial the public information office just as Sally drops off a small cardboard to-go box, chopsticks and a fortune cookie on my desk.

"Hi, this is Lisa Powers with KWLF Radio in Chandler," I say into the phone, giving Sally a five-dollar bill and mouthing thanks. "Do you have a minute to answer some questions about getting a fishing license?"

"Sure, but most of the info is online."

"Yes, I read through most of that. But what I want to know… do you track licenses? Is there a way to know where the licensed holder might be fishing at any given time?"

"No," the man replies. "The license number is used to track license purchases, big game applications and bonus points."

"So, those fishing don't have to show their license before they go to a specific lake? No one records the time in and out?"

"No, but a ranger can ask anyone for their license at any time, and if they don't produce it, they're fined. What's this really about?" he asks, a little perturbed.

"I was trying to find out where a specific person went fishing a while back, but I think I'm at a dead end. Thanks for your help."

I hang up, frustration showing on my face. I manipulate the chopsticks to eat a bite of snow peas and shrimp, deep in thought.

The haunting sounds of the "Murder in the Air Mystery Theatre" theme song plays and fades under as my voice starts.

"Finally, Liz and Brad are reunited and out of the 'Frightful Fun House.' Were special effects really used? Or was it a cover for murder?"

Sounds of a TV news program fade in, and Ron's voice as the announcer begins. "An elderly woman is found dead inside the Frightful Fun House at the Davidson Amusements Carnival. Police are not sure if she died of natural causes or if foul play was involved. A young couple found the woman presumably deceased inside the Fun House, but were later told by carnival organizers it was just a special effect. However, other carnival-goers discovered her body not long after and notified police. She is identified as..." The man's voice trails off.

"How could I have believed those people?" a dejected Brad asks.

"You didn't know, Brad," Liz replies softly.

"Were they trying to cover it up, or do they have so many plants they didn't realize the old lady wasn't one of them?" Brad asks.

"That's what the medical examiner is trying to figure out now," Liz says. "Let's hope they find—" Her cell phone ringing startles Liz. "Hello?" she answers. "Yes? I see...oh goodness, that's too bad...okay, thanks for calling." Liz closes her phone and drops her head.

"What?" Brad asks.

"That was the detective. She says the woman was in town for a quilt show, and just happened upon the carnival. She apparently went to the fun house by herself, and when she got into the Insanitorium where the freaks were...she apparently died of a heart attack. She was literally scared to death."

"Oh, man," says Brad. "That is awful."

"They're still going to do an autopsy," Liz explains. "Maybe they'll find out she had a weak heart or something. Since we were two of the last people to see her, the detective said we might get a call from the medical examiner...and maybe her insurance company."

"Great," Brad says facetiously. "This is so bizarre. I just want this to be o—"

"What did you say?" Liz interrupts. "Oh my gosh, I just remembered! I saw a little man working a calculator in a room off the hallway, but when I thought he was going to help me, instead, he closed and locked the door between us. Later on when I looked back down the hall to his door, it wasn't there anymore—it was just a plain wall. Do you s'pose there's any connection?"

"I don't know, Liz, but are you sure that really happened?"

"Of course I'm sure, I just forgot all about him until just now. I need to call the detective back!"

"Does the little man know something about the elderly woman's death? Perhaps he had something to do with it? Find out next time on 'Murder in the Air Mystery Theatre.' I'm Lauren Price. Thanks for listening."

CHAPTER 10

THURSDAY, APRIL 18

Harry follows me to the station, each in our respective vehicles. I hit a speed dial number on my cell phone while driving and listen to the earpiece. A message machine comes on, but I sing the "Happy Birthday" song to my mom.

"Love you, Mom. Hope you're having a great day."

I pull into the radio station parking lot and my cell phone rings.

"Hey, Joe, whatcha workin' today?"

I park my car, grab my bags and wave to Harry as he watches me enter the back door.

"I know you're not supposed to be on the Dwayne Meyers cold case, but just FYI...we got a hit from that crime scene investigator in Texas," Johnstone begins. "He thinks he's going to have something for us on the duct tape."

"That's great, Joe. When?" I dump my bag on the desk, sink into my chair and grab a notepad and pen.

"You reporters. Always on deadline. I don't know, we'll get it when we get it."

"Hey, can't blame a girl for asking."

"I know. He said maybe next week."

I hear Johnstone dig around on papers on his desk. "Oh, and I got the name of that nail polish you asked about." Joe seemed a little embarrassed to talk about what, in his mind, was akin to a feminine product.

"Great, what is it?" I ask.

"Arson made a copy of what was left of the label and blew it up, but it's still a little hard to read. Looks like 'Peru-B some-thing.'"

I look down my list of the popular nail polish company's creative color names.

"Could it be 'Peru-B-Ruby?'"

There's a pause while Joe strains to read the print. "Yeah, might be. Why?"

I'm not sure how much to tell him just yet. "It may be nothing, but I talked to the salon where Rosemary went, and turns out she had a standing appointment every two weeks."

"Yeah, so?"

Men. "So, it means she had her nails done on a regular basis, so why would she be doing them at home? Also, the salon said the name of her favorite polish was called 'Color So Hot it Berns'– that's b-*e*-r-n-s."

"So, she changed her polish. Not against the law, ya know."

"I know, but—"

"But what? Tell me what you're thinking."

"Sure, she could've chipped a nail and was fixing it. But she would most likely have the exact same color the salon used. What if..." I pause and take a breath. "What if someone planted the polish, spread a lot of fingernail polish remover around her, lit it and took off?"

There's another pause, this time from Joe's side of the phone.

"That's quite a theory." Joe's voice lowers. "If someone's leaking information to you from Fire, they could be in big trouble."

"That's not the case. You saying the arson team found an accelerant?"

"I'd rather you get that directly from Fire. They're taking the lead on this now."

"Okay, how about the M.E.'s report? Dr. Douglas told me it could be eight weeks before the details are released. If an accelerant is found, can you guys get it pushed up?"

"That's possible, but I don't think we've got enough yet."

I take a big breath. "What if...you added possible murder by cyanide poisoning covered up by a fire?"

"Janet, it's Lisa from KWLF Radio."

"I don't think we have anything more to talk about," Janet says coldly.

"Well, I'm not sure about that, Janet. You see, I've found out a little more information about your relationship with Tyler Jameson, and I think you may know something more about Rosemary's death."

There's a pause, and an unexpected chuckle. "Now, Lisa, I know you're young and all, but you just can't go around saying things like that," Janet says in a sickening sweet tone. "I know our conversation didn't end on the most positive note the other day, so, perhaps we should meet again and see if we can't work all this out?"

Yes, I think. *Gotcha.* "I guess we could. Any particular place?"

"You know where the lakes are off Fulton Ranch Road? There's a lovely spot with a little gazebo on the south side about halfway in. How about tonight, say around, oh, seven o'clock? Maybe we'll catch the sunset, too."

"That will be just fine, thanks."

A blazing orange sun sinks in the western Valley skies, creating a glorious mixture of lavender, yellow, blue and pink over the southern Chandler treetops. I park my car by the stone gazebo, which is shaded by large mesquite trees. Cranes, blue herons and other birds stand like statues along the human-made lake, waiting patiently for their dinner. I spot Janet sitting alone on a seat inside the open structure.

I turn off my engine and reach into the glove compartment for the baggie of white cyanide powder, and unwrap it from its tissue disguise. I leave my car keys on the seat. *In case I need to make a quick exit.*

I ease out of my car, ribs still a bit tender. My body casting long shadows, I approach Janet cautiously. The only sound is the gentle whooshing of waves in a nearby rock waterfall.

Janet stands, wearing a forced smile and holding her purse tight.

"So, Lisa, what is it you believe I know about Rosemary's death?" Janet begins. "And be careful what you—"

"I think you killed her," I interrupt.

Janet blinks a few times and the color drains from her face. She takes a big breath and starts walking toward me. "Now see here—"

I hold up the plastic packet. "Why would you have cyanide in your purse, Janet? Perhaps to poison Rosemary, then set a fire with fingernail polish remover to try to cover it up?"

Janet's eyes grow wide. "So *you* stole it!" she sneers.

"And you didn't just have a passing relationship with Tyler Jameson, did you, Janet? You were in love with him, weren't you, but he didn't love you back."

"Why, you little..." Janet's hand comes out of her purse with a fishing knife, and she rushes toward me. "Aaagh!" she screeches as she lunges forward, dropping her purse on the pavers in the process.

I jump to one side and fall to my knees as Janet stumbles past me. Janet turns back around, waving the knife slowly back and forth. I cautiously get to my feet, grimacing with pain and holding my ribs.

"You're not such a hotshot reporter after all. You'll never know how Tyler and I felt about each other. We were going to be together once Rosemary was outta the way." She stalks slowly, a maniacal look on her face.

"Janet, don't do this," I plead, backing away. "I'm sure the D.A. will go easy on you, this being your first offense—"

"Ha! Without you, they won't know a thing, you stupid bitch!" Janet thrusts the sharp blade once again at me. I duck my head and roll across the concrete paver flooring, wincing in pain. I scramble to my feet and back up toward the ledge as Janet wheels around and runs toward me with surprising speed. I dive for Janet's purse and swing it around, catching the arm carrying the dagger. The force spins Janet off balance, pushing her over the gazebo railing and into the lake with a splash. Herons, ducks and other waterfowl flutter and squawk in surprise.

"Police! Hold it right there!" Three officers with weapons drawn rush into the shelter as I drop onto the bench seat, panting.

"Jeez, no rush," I say to Detective Johnstone, who brings up the rear. He waves to the officers to retrieve a sputtering Janet from the shallow water. I toss the baggie of poison to him, brush off my clothes and limp back to my car.

ANNOUNCER LIVE:
In a startling turn of events, the fiery death of a local heiress turns out to be murder and arson. KWLF's Lisa Powers reports on this exclusive story:

LISA VOICEOVER:
Janet Fradley almost got away with murder.

Chandler Police say the local woman and would-be socialite confessed to killing pharmaceutical heir Rosemary Thornton with cyanide and covering it up by setting a fire with fingernail polish remover. However, Detective Joe Johnstone says she may not have acted alone.

JOHNSTONE SOUND ON TAPE:
"We have also arrested Ms. Thornton's third husband, Tyler Jameson, on suspicion of first-degree murder. A Chandler Fire Department arson team discovered a series of booby-traps, allegedly set by Jameson, that went off and caused a series of fires in the couple's home while he was reportedly on a fishing trip."

LISA VOICEOVER:
In light of the new information, a rush was put on the Thornton autopsy results. While the medical examiner says bodies of tobacco smokers also contain some cyanide, the murder victim's cyanide levels were ten times the normal amount.

Police are not yet certain whether Jameson and Fradley worked together or independently to kill Thornton early last week when her mansion erupted in flames. Fradley claims the two were going to Brazil together, but an airline ticket—scheduled for next week and found in Jameson's truck—was a single one-way fare to Costa Rica.

For KWLF radio, I'm Lisa Powers.

ANNOUNCER LIVE:

And in a related event, police have also charged Fradley with assault and attempted murder of KWLF radio reporter Lisa Powers. A plate of cookies given to Powers by Fradley was determined by an area drug-testing lab to also contain cyanide. In addition, Fradley threatened Powers with a knife prior to her arrest last night. Powers was not harmed. Both Fradley and Jameson remain in the Maricopa County jail, each with a one million dollar bond.

Mysterious music begins.

"On the previous 'Murder in the Air Mystery Theatre,' Liz recalls her encounter with a calculating man, and wonders if he has something do to with the old woman's death," my voice reads. *"Meanwhile, a private investigator representing the woman's insurance company meets with Liz and Brad."*

"So, you say she was already cold to the touch?" he asks.

"Well, cool, anyway," Brad answers. "Not warm, for sure."

"That just means she may have been dead for a while when you found her," he explains. "What about the expression on her face? What can you tell me about it?"

"Well, I don't really remember...I guess she looked like she was...surprised."

"I think it was more like shock," Liz says. "Her eyes were huge, her mouth was wide open, like she was trying to scream or something. But I guess if I was having a heart attack, I'd probably be both sur-

prised and shocked. That is what the medical examiner found, Isn't it?"

"Well, actually, there have been some new developments," the PI says. "Turns out a month before, when the carnival was in Ohio, there was another unexplained death, also in the Frightful Fun House. Police are trying to get that body exhumed so they can do another autopsy and see if any similarities are found."

"Oh my god," Liz says. "That's terrible!"

"Just one more question, Brad," the PI says. "You say the woman was clutching her heart when you found her?"

"Uh, yeah, I think so," he tries to recall.

"Wait a sec, Brad. Remember when you tried to feel for a pulse. You bent over to see if she was breathing, and that's when you touched her hand. Wasn't her hand closer to her throat?"

"Oh, uh, yeah, maybe you're right," Brad says. "But what difference does that make?"

"Well, while it initially looked like she had a heart attack, the medical examiner found traces of a lethal drug in the dead woman's blood."

The 'Murder in the Air Mystery Theatre' theme music soars as my voice comes in.

"What kind of a drug was discovered in the body of the old quilter? Will the same drug show up in the exhumed body? And who would've given done such a thing? There's a lot more on 'Murder in the Air Mystery Theatre' next time. I'm Lauren Price. Good night."

CHAPTER 11

FRIDAY, APRIL 19

It's early afternoon, and the newsroom is fairly quiet. Grant's chair sits empty while David cleans equipment. The only activity happens at the newsroom secretary's desk, where she responds to constant calls about the Janet Fradley sting operation and arrest.

"Yes, thank you for calling, I'll pass the message to Lisa," she says raising her eyebrows toward the young reporter.

I mouth thank you and straighten up my area, gathering scripts and notes from my most recent stories and filing them in folders.

I pick up the cold case file, and not seeing Grant around, dial the phone.

"Hey, Joe, just thought I'd check on that duct tape test before the weekend. Anything?" There's a long pause as I listen intently on the newsroom phone. "Joe? What's up?"

"Uh, probably nothing really."

I detect something strange in Johnstone's voice. "Now that doesn't sound good," I say.

FADE OUT · 183

"It's just that...well, they're redoing the test again, and we should have final results Monday."

"Well, that's good, right? So he was able to find prints?"

"Yes, but..." Joe answers cautiously. "Look, I've got a staff meeting..."

"Whoa, hold on, Joe. Do you have some preliminary information?"

"Sorry, kiddo, I am not at liberty to discuss that." Joe's voice suddenly gets brusque and businesslike. "On a related note, ballistics is testing the new bullets today."

"Let me watch, Joe. You owe me, after I helped you put Janet in jail."

Johnstone hesitates. "Hey, I thought this case was still off-limits."

"Well, technically it is, but I think I can get Grant to let me cover this part of it."

"Well, okay, but only if you get approval. They'll be running them this afternoon at 3 out at the range. Harry can drive you out, but you don't pull any stunts like ditching him or getting into anyone else's car, got it?"

"No problem, Joe, thanks!"

Excitement bursts inside me as I glance at my watch but the eagerness fades. *Can I convince Grant to let me go?*

I start to dial Grant's cell phone when my cell phone rings. Caller ID says Erickson, Bruce. I sigh and press "answer."

"Hey, Bruce, how are you?"

I close my eyes, listening to an obvious rant on the other end.

"Yes, I'm fine, Bruce, I—" I'm interrupted by the news anchor. "Bruce, really, I was surrounded by officers the entire time."

I listen for a moment. "I appreciate your concern, but—" I'm interrupted again. "Tonight?" I grimace. "Uh, sorry, but I'm sitting in on ballistics testing of the cold case bullets this afternoon, and I don't know how long it will take. But..." I take a big breath. "Well, there is a possibility...I mean, I wondered if you...and me, of course...could get together sometime with my friend Ron and my landlady Evelyn?"

I wait for a response. "Not really a 'double date,' just, ya know...coffee or lunch." A pause. "Saturday? Like tomorrow?" My eyes open wide. "Um, sure, let me check with them and see if they are available, and I'll get back to you. Uh-huh, thanks again, Bruce. Bye."

The arrangements made for the four of us to meet at a local 24-hour restaurant, I check my bag to make sure all my recording gear is in place. I call Grant's phone again, but he doesn't pick up.

"Hey, Grant, it's me, Lisa, and I know I'm technically not supposed to be working on the cold case, but I couldn't find you and they're doing testing on the bullets this afternoon and it's a great opportunity, and I know I can get lots of good sound and after all I'll be with Harry and all kinds of police officers so I'll be safe, so, yeah, that's where I'll be, I hope it's okay." I quickly hang up and stare at the phone for a moment, breathing once again.

Sally, the newsroom secretary, walks over to my desk with a stack of pink call slips.

"These are just from the last two hours," she says, waving them in front of me.

"Sorry 'bout that, Sally," I say apologetically.

"Oh, no problem. Listeners just want to make sure you're all right." She shuffles through the messages. "But I've had a couple of calls from young teens, thinking what an exciting job you must have and asking how they can get into radio." Harry Dugan lumbers into the newsroom as she continues. "Oh, get this, I even had one caller ask if I knew how he could buy that guy's ticket to Costa Rica!"

"Sheesh, that's a new one," I reply, waving to Harry. "Hey, I'm heading out with Harry to watch ballistics testing. I left a message for Grant. If you see him, tell him I'll probably just go home after that."

"Sounds good," Sally answers. "You just be careful, okay?"

"Yes, ma'am, I will!" I pick up my bag, take one more look at my neat desk and wave goodbye. Harry escorts me out.

The police department firing range is set far out in the desert, several miles south of the city limits, and shared by several area law enforcement agencies. It's the same location where police detonate explosive devices, old ammo and other unstable seized contraband found in the course of their jobs.

Security waves Harry and me through the gate, and he parks the car. We're ushered through security and led to a door that simply labeled "Ballistics."

"I'll be right here," Harry says, nodding to a small waiting room with chairs, a coffee table and magazines.

I enter an enormous warehouse-type room with soundproofing on every surface. Several large, silver metal rectangular boxes border the room, and I spot Sgt. Hoffman with another police officer standing at one.

"Hi, Sergeant," I say, approaching the two. "Detective Johnstone said I could observe today."

Hoffman looks up from a clipboard with paperwork. "Lisa Powers, this is Lt. Schroder, who will do the examinations today. He's one of the top forensic ballistics experts in the Valley."

Schroder and I shake hands and exchange pleasantries, and the lieutenant gives me a David Clark headset, with thick leather-like head and ear pads.

Schroder finishes loading a couple of weapons, which I recognize as a typical Glock service revolver and another similar gun.

"What is that weapon?" I ask.

"It's a Beretta Px4 Storm. Similar in shape and size to the Glock, but might give us some different firing results. All right, headsets on."

Schroder and Hoffman put the noise reduction earpieces on, and I follow suit. Schroder picks up the Glock and places it into a small, round hole at the top of the metal testing unit. He glances at Hoffman, who nods in return.

Schroder fires. Even with protective gear, the "boom" is loud from inside the chamber, and I jump. The men look at me, and I smile sheepishly, giving a thumbs-up sign that I'm okay. *Crap, forgot to hit Record.* I get my gear set up properly.

Lt. Schroder pulls his headsets down on his shoulders, and lifts the top off the ballistics chamber, filled with water. He locates the spent bullet and picks it out with a large set of tongs. He and Sgt. Hoffman peer at it briefly. He carries it to a large table with a computer, and a microscope fitted with a camera attached through one eyepiece. Six large, flat-screen monitors hang side by side on the wall behind, all showing black screens. Schroder places the bullet on one of a series of flat glass plates laid out beside the 'scope. He marks the plate with some handwritten information and returns to the firing chamber.

"We'll do it again to get a comparison," he states, putting his headsets back in place, picking up the Glock and firing it into the metal container again.

They repeat the process, taking the fired slugs to the glass plate, noting info on each. Schroder does the same with the Beretta. Finally, they have a number of bullets to compare.

"You have the old images?" Schroder asks Hoffman, who pulls out a small envelope from his pocket and produces a flash drive. Schroder puts it into a USB port and in a few seconds, extreme close-up images flash on the first flat screen.

"Okay, now we'll photograph each one," Schroder announces.

Looking at the older images, the lieutenant takes the first spent shell and turns it around in his hands, looking carefully from each direction. He lays it back on the glass and slides it under the microscope lens. The shell appears on the same computer screen as a huge image under the other one. He snaps macro shots of each piece of metal through the scope lens until one by one they appear on the monitor.

"So, is this where you compare the test bullets to the ones found at the cold case crime scene?" I ask, holding my microphone toward the ballistics expert.

"Right," says Schroder, intent on selecting an old and a new image from each weapon. With the computer mouse, he pulls two images from the corners, resizing them so they are identical in shape, and places them side-by-side on the monitor.

"So what are you looking for specifically?" I peer at the small, misshapen globs of torn metal.

"There are class characteristics of a particular type of gun, such as the Glock or the Beretta, as well as individual characteristics unique to a particular firearm," Schroder explains. "You can see some striations in each bullet. Those are the fine grooves etched into the shell by the firing of the weapon."

Schroder drags one image over the other, and they are almost an exact match.

"Wow, so the same gun shot both those bullets?" I exclaim.

"Not so fast. We're dealing with internal ballistics at the moment. We can tell these were both shot by a Glock because the flat sides of the octagonal-shaped barrel perform the rifling. There are many other things to take into consideration as well, such as velocity, energy and trajectory when we study external ballistics. But what we're really searching for are those unique markings that might indicate it's the same weapon."

Schroder takes a laser pointer and aims it at the photo of the older bullet.

"See all those very fine marks? Often a criminal will try to change the characteristics of their weapon. In this case, it looks like they rubbed the interior of the gun with a steel brush, which actually makes it very distinctive."

He goes to another spent casing, this one from George Ware's car and puts it under the microscope's camera lens. When he focuses, they see the same fine markings.

"Hey, there they are again. It's a match!" I am excited about the findings.

"It's a good chance this might be the same weapon, but again, there are so many variables. It has to hold up in court and go beyond 'reasonable doubt.'"

The "Murder In The Air" theme music comes full, and fades under. My voice begins.

"Last time on 'Murder in the Air Mystery Theatre,' authorities find a drug in the dead quilter's system. They also discover she wasn't the first death for the carnival company."

"It's called 'succinylcholine,'" the private investigator explains, *"and it mimics the symptoms of a heart attack. It's a strong muscle relaxant that paralyzes the respiratory muscles. It's usually used in hospitals to insert a breathing tube into the throat of a patient who is still conscious. In higher doses, it can paralyze the entire breathing apparatus, and the victim slowly suffocates to death."*

"Why didn't they find it earlier?" Brad asks.

"It's not normally tested for in toxicology screens, so that's why they missed it the first time," the PI answers. "But the DB in the Ohio

case—an older man in his 60s—turned up with the same lethal dose when they exhumed the body."

"Those poor people," Liz says. "Who would do that to them?"

"It's got to be someone who works for the carnival," Brad interjects. "But why?"

"Here's my theory," the PI explains. "In the first few days of the carnival's opening in Ohio, attendance was lagging. But after the death in the Fun House, and word spread, they had throngs of people buying tickets. I think someone did it to boost interest in the carnival."

"What about that carny guy who sold us the tickets to the fun house?" Liz asks. "He gave me the creeps."

The pages of a small pad rustle. "That would be Alvin 'Big Al' Saccowitz, who's been with Davidson Amusements for about 15 years. He knows the Frightful Fun House inside and out, and is always coming up with new, scarier things to include."

"Who else do you suspect?" Brad asks.

"Well, there's Tonya Moreland, the carnival's publicist," the PI continues. "Guess she's always trying wacky things to attract people, but she's almost too obvious."

"What about the little man I saw in the room?" Liz asks. "He must've been a bookkeeper or something. He had ledgers on his desk and was working furiously at a calculator. And when he saw me, he quickly shut a drawer on the left side of his desk. I really did see him. Has anyone been able to find him?"

"As a matter of fact," the PI says, "I think we located someone who meets that description. Ben Brooks, 62, a seemingly mild-mannered accountant for the carnival owner. He's worked with them for only about five years."

"So, what's the next step?" Brad asks.

"I think police have enough to at least bring them in for questioning. Meanwhile, the carnival's been shut down, so they're not going anywhere."

My voice comes in over the "Murder in the Air" theme music.

"The plot thickens as police peruse the possible persons presumed to be part of this plan. Be back here next time to learn more about the suspects on 'Murder in the Air Mystery Theatre.' I'm Lauren Price. Good night."

CHAPTER 12

SATURDAY, APRIL 20

An awkward pause follows introductions between Bruce, Ron, Evelyn and me as we settle into a garish chartreuse-and-pink corner booth at Cactus Joe's. It's shortly after noon, and the restaurant is bustling with patrons chatting at every other table—except ours.

Ron nervously smoothes and resmoothes his tie as he sits next to Evelyn. She wears a soft print dress. I'm in blue jeans and T-shirt, and am a bit uncomfortable with Bruce so close to my side, especially when he's better dressed than me, with a starched button-down shirt and dress pants. We all shuffle silverware and sigh collective relief when a waitress comes to the table to hand out menus.

"Afternoon, folks, what can I start you with? Coffee, iced tea, soda?"

Ron and I order coffee, Bruce gets lemonade and Evelyn requests hot tea. The server leaves, and the four of us soundlessly review the food offerings. Evelyn puts down her menu and finally breaks the silence.

"So, Lisa, how are those little kitties of yours?"

"Oh, I'm still looking for a home for them, but they're fine. Really adorable. They're starting to move around now."

There's another uncomfortable gap. Ron fidgets with his fingers. "So, how did the ballistics testing go?" he asks me.

I lean forward excitedly toward my older friend. "It was so cool. They have this huge reinforced metal chamber they shoot bullets into. They get extreme close-up photos through a microscope of what remains of the shell and compare them to determine the type."

I pause as the waitress delivers the beverages, and we all order lunch.

"So, any matches?" Ron asks, pouring cream into his coffee.

"Turns out some of the bullets pulled out of Denise's house and George Ware's car were completely different, and they're running them through the registry. But other slugs seem to be an exact match to the ones found at the scene of the cold case...possibly indicating an old weapon and a newer one were used."

Bruce and Evelyn squirm in their seats, uncomfortable hearing this conversation.

"That means the incidents are related to the Meyers death, right?" Ron asks.

"That's what Sgt. Hoffman believes, so we just have to figure out how they're conn..."

"Ahem." Bruce clears his throat. "Hey, do you have to talk shop? Don't you get enough of that five days a week?"

194 · LAURIE FAGEN

"Oh, sorry," I reply. "What would you like to talk about?"

"Well, we..."

"I watch you every weekend," Evelyn blurts out to Bruce, her cheeks turning pink. Her eyelashes flutter at the anchor. "You always look so...handsome."

"Oh, thank you, Evelyn, that's kind of you to say." Bruce puffs up a bit at the attention.

"I just loved that story you did about the new baby bear at the Phoenix Zoo," Evelyn continues. "What kind was it again?"

"Thanks, it was an Andean Bear cub. The zoo is doing a contest to name the little guy. Oh, and they just had a Spectacled Owl chick born, too. It's almost all white with black markings around its eyes."

Ron pipes up. "Hey, Lisa, remember when you did that story about the brown pelican and he almost dive-bombed you?"

"Yeah, I had no idea those birds were so big!"

We all share a laugh, before silence hits again. Another timely appearance by the server to deliver our food saves us.

As the "Murder In The Air" theme music comes full, sounds of a busy police department fade in, with telephones jangling, people talking, wheeled chairs rolling.

"Please, take a seat, Mr. Sac-co-witz, is that it?" a male police detective asks.

"It's Sac-co-witz, Alvin, but you can just call me Big Al," Saccowitz says in a booming voice. "I have no idea why I'm here, but I imagine you're going to tell me."

"*Indeed,*" the detective says. "*So, Big Al, where do you get your ideas for the scary things you have inside that fun house of yours?*"

"*Oh, well, a variety of places,*" Al says. "*I keep in touch with other carnies, find out the latest and greatest...and make a few up of my own,*" he says proudly.

"*So, what'd ya do before you joined the circus?*" the detective asks.

"*I was a veterinarian for a number of years, but I found I prefer life on the road.*"

"*So, you've used syringes to give shots to those animals in the past, right?*"

"*Well, yes, of course,*" Big Al answers.

"*Is it true you are able to get real eyeballs and guts from dead animals to put in your show?*"

Big Al pauses. "*I do not know who you are talking with, but all my props are absolutely the highest quality and obtained legally.*"

"*Do ya ever get into contests with your fellow carnies in Davidson Amusements to see who can bring in the most suckers?*" the detective asks.

"*Now, now, we call them our customers, and yes, my Frightful Fun House is typically in the top five attractions for Davidson Amusement...and we rank as one of the best in the country,*" he says a bit pompously.

"*How long ago was that ranking, Mr. Saccowitz?*"

There's a pause.

"*Uh, well, it was just a few years ago...let me think, maybe 1998?*"

"*Hmmm, that was more than 13 years ago,*" the detective notes. "*But murder would be a good way to get those ratings up, now wouldn't it?*"

"I would never resort to anything of the kind!" he sputters. "The Davidson Amusement Carnival is my family!"

"You can go, Mr. Saccowitz," says the detective, "but don't leave town."

There are sound effects of the big man's chair scraping wood as he gets up, his footsteps heading to the door, and the door opening and closing as he leaves the room. Within seconds, there are more footsteps going toward the door, and the interrogation room door opens again. Off mic, the male detective calls out, "Ms. Moreland."

Sounds of clicking stiletto heels fade in as Tonya Moreland enters the room and sits down.

"Thanks for coming down, Ms. Moreland," the detective says. "I understand you do publicity for the carnival?"

"More precisely, I am in public relations and marketing," Tonya replies with a bit of an air and a thick Bronx accent.

"Is it true you have diabetes, Ms. Moreland?"

"Well, yes, as a matter of fact, I do," she answers, surprised.

"So, you know a fair amount about giving shots with syringes, I s'pose?" the detective asks.

"I have to inject myself with insulin several times a day, that is true."

"Really? And, I hear you've come up with some—shall we say 'interesting'—ways of getting people to come to your shindig, is that true?"

"Well, many consider them to be highly effective PR campaigns with solid advertising," she responds.

"Was it your idea to have an eyeball-eating contest where the contestants ate peeled grapes with chopsticks?"

"Yeah, it was, and it was very successful," she answers proudly. "Same with the 'eat the most maggots' competitions using cooked rice and a little water. People loved it."

"What about injecting old people with a drug to make it look like they were scared to death? That your idea, too?" the detective queried.

"No, of course not!" Tonya answered vehemently. "I am a professional!"

"Yeah, well, that's all for now, but don't go buying any plane tickets."

Her high-heeled pumps click quickly out of the room.

"Bring in the bookkeeper," the detective barks.

There's a soft shuffling of a small man's shoes, and the scraping of the chair as it pulls up to the table.

"So, Mr. Brooks, is it?" the detective asks.

"Uh, yes, I mean, yes sir, uh, I'm Benjamin B. Brooks, certified public accountant for Davidson Amusements," the little man stammers.

"So, I see you've been with a lot of different carnival outfits. Why'd ya run away with the circus, what, three decades ago? What's the attraction?" the detective inquires.

"Well, I got tired of all the whining and complaining by my co-workers that they wanted to travel but never had the time or money to do it. I wanted to show them that it could be done," he said with a touch of arrogance.

"And exactly what kinda office did you work in?"

"It was a medical supply office, and we ordered all kinds of supplies for doctors' and dentists' offices."

"So, I s'pose you handled rubber gloves, those wooden sticks for the tongue, that kinda stuff?"

"Yes, of course," Ben answers.

"What did you do with the syringes?"

"I would surely...uh, I mean, I would make sure to...uh...to never touch them," he says adamantly, realizing where the questioning is going.

"Is that right, Brooks?" the detective responds. "We're done here—for the moment. But just make sure you don't go doing any traveling for the next week or so."

The "mystery theatre" theme music starts. My voice starts:

"So, who's the one who would kill to see more attendance at the carnival? Is it the haughty high-heeled hack with hypodermics who hatched wacky ways to wangle would-be patrons? Maybe it's the mild-mannered numbers man who made his money at a medical offi-ffice? Or the veteran veterinarian and expert vaccinator with the loud voice who valued vulgar viscera?

"Stay tuned when the next 'Murder in the Air Mystery Theatre' podcast continues. I'm Lauren Price, thanks for listening."

CHAPTER 13

MONDAY, APRIL 22

I sweep into the newsroom first thing Monday morning, dumping my recording bag and file folders on my desk. Tossing down my sunglasses, I pick up a coffee cup and head for the kitchen when I notice an odd silence. I look up to see Sally watching me, looking worried and nervous. David lowers his eyes quickly, giving particular attention to an equipment-cleaning project. Grant rises from his desk, and solemnly heads toward me. *Uh-oh, not again.*

"Now what did I do?" My eyes search Grant's face for some clue.

"We need to go to the conference room."

I feel as if I'm being led to my execution. My brain scrambles for an answer. *Okay, a lot has happened in the past few days. The sting with Janet. Janet and Tyler arrested. Ballistics testing. Something to do with that stupid administrative leave? Grant must not have liked my message from Friday.*

Grant opens the door to the meeting room for me, and there's Mr. Tompkins, the station manager, with Detective Johnstone, looking very grim. As I walk into the room, around the corner of the large wooden table is an older man in an expensive gray suit sitting next to Tompkins, with Sgt. Hoffman, and next to him, a sturdy woman with short blonde hair wearing her daytime blue cop uniform. I spot the small four-star pins on both collars and recognize her as the newly hired Chandler chief of police. I gulp. *Oh boy, something is really up.*

"Good morning, Lisa," the woman says with a calming smile. "I'm Sharon Masterson, Chandler police chief. Have a seat, please."

Grant and I take our chairs. Johnstone is acting as if he is deeply engrossed in the thick manila file in front of him, the older man is pulling papers out of his open briefcase on the table and Hoffman has a yellow pad and pen, like he's ready to take notes.

Tompkins clasps his hands on top of the table. "Now, Lisa, this has to do with that cold case you've been covering. As we all know, you have become very close to this story, in fact, you've become part of the story. But, we also have First Amendment rights here, which is why Larry Stevens, the station's legal counsel, is here."

"I need a lawyer?" My eyes open wide. *Maybe I need to call Nate. Wonder if he could represent—*

"No, no, my dear," Tompkins chuckles. "You've done nothing wrong. We just want to make sure you and the story are protected."

"Wait...I don't understand. What's going on?"

"It's a very sensitive issue, Lisa," the police chief says softly. "Just try to relax."

I take a big breath as Detective Johnstone opens his file.

"Lisa, we need to ask you a few more questions about your conversation with George Ware that day before the accident."

"Sure. You've got my statement from Harry Dugan, right?"

"Yes, but that was only a few days after your release from the hospital. There've been some...new developments that we want to check out."

"Of course, how can I help?"

"Tell us what you remember about the conversation with Mr. Ware."

I went over George's story, about his watching the pick-up site for more than 24 hours, having to go to the bathroom, and coming back to find his partner shot dead.

"He felt like it was his fault, just because he left for a minute," I conclude.

"Was that the only reason he felt responsible?"

I close my eyes as my memory goes back to that day. *Think, think.* "When I first got in the car, I could smell alcohol so strongly, I offered to drive. But he said 'Nuthin' wrong with me...just like I had nuthin' to do with bungling that money pickup.' That was in my statement, right?"

"Yes, it was. Anything else you recall? Was his conscience bothering him?"

"I really don't think he was a part of..." I stop, remembering. "Wait, he said something about later hearing whispers and getting dirty looks...as if *he* was involved."

Johnstone glances at the chief.

"It seemed he knew what the other officers were thinking, but he didn't say the words, I did: 'It was an inside job.' He didn't confirm or deny. I'm so sorry, I think it was right before we crashed. I don't believe I included it earlier."

"That's okay, it's why we're here." The chief nods at Johnstone and Hoffman. "I think that does it." She pulls away from the table and starts to leave.

Wait a minute, this doesn't make sense! I want to scream. "Hold on, I don't get it. Joe, you said you'd have ballistics and fingerprint test results today. And what about linguistics on those notes and the ransom call?"

The public information officer looks at Chief Masterson for direction.

"Just the basics, Joe," she says, turning to Grant and me. "But, this is off-the-record and not for broadcast, do I make myself clear?"

"Now, wait a minute, Chief," Tompkins rises. "The public has a right to know if an officer of the law is involved—"

"Terry, don't push me," she says sternly, but backs off. "Look, it's all going to hit the fan soon enough. I'm just asking for 24 hours so we can make sure we're ready."

Tompkins looks at the attorney, who nods in agreement.

"Fair enough," Tompkins replies.

"So, I'm back on the cold case, right?" I eagerly ask Grant once we've returned to the newsroom.

Grant slowly shakes his head side to side. "You certainly are persistent and focused. But you must keep me in the loop on everything with this case, you understand? As the chief said, it's very sensitive, especially if one of their own is involved. It goes without saying we always want to have our stories accurate, but this particular one demands double and triple fact checking. I also want to know who you're talking to, and you take Dugan with you whenever you go out."

I open my mouth to object.

"And no arguing," he adds.

"Okay, got it."

"So what are you working on next?"

"I got clearance to speak with an FBI agent who's an expert in forensic linguistics. I'm hoping he can discuss the original ransom call as well as all the notes Denise has received over the past decades. I've got an interview set at 2 today in our conference room."

"Anything else?"

"Just wait for PD to release their statement. I'll put together a draft of the story after I talk to the FBI guy, then I should be able to drop in the details and we'll be ready to go. I'll give it to you to read over before we air it, okay?"

"Yes, please." Grant pauses. "You know, we're walking a fine line here between freedom of information, the public's right to know, and the government restricting access to records." He takes a slow sip of his coffee. "We've worked hard here in Arizona to be part of the checks and balances of government. When challenges to secrecy are successful, the news is better and so is the government. Thing is, we'll give 'em their 24 hours, but no more. Then we run with the story."

Sally shows a tall, well-dressed man into the radio station's boardroom, now cleared of everything except me, my recorder, a mic and my reporter's notepad.

"Lisa, this is Special Agent Alexander," Sally says before quietly closing the door behind her.

"Nice to meet you, sir." I shake his hand, noting a firm grip and very soft skin.

"Good to meet you, too. You can call me Geoff." He takes a seat in front of the mic and opens a large, well-worn leather notebook, spreading it out in front of him. He pulls an expensive-looking pen out of an interior pocket in his dark suit jacket, places it in front of him and folds his hands together and looks at me.

"I must say you and your operation apparently have great influence in this town. Media interviews with FBI agents are rarely granted, and even less often regarding specific cases, but here we are. Where would you like to begin?"

I blush slightly. I press the Record button and a red light glows. "I do appreciate your time. First of all, please spell your name and tell me your official title with the FBI."

"My name is Geoffrey—that's G-e-o-f-f-r-e-y Alexander, common spelling, and I am a special agent, assigned to the FBI's Phoenix Field Office of Violent Crime and Major Offender Squad."

"Thanks. And I understand you are the coordinator for the National Center for the Analysis of Violent Crime for Arizona? What does that entail?"

"I am the liaison with local law enforcement agencies when they request behavioral analysis and profiling services from the FBI's NCAVC. This can include not only linguistic analysis of communications, but other types of behavioral analysis on cases involving crimes against children and crimes against adults."

"So, what exactly is Forensic Linguistic Analysis?"

"It's the study and examination of written and spoken communications—such as letters, texts, emails, voicemails, manifestos, ransom notes, threats or any other kind of communication—to gain information about the author. We use a set of linguistic tools that help investigators analyze and determine the identity of the speaker or writer."

"How hard is that to do?" I ask.

Alexander smiles. "It's impossible for humans to communicate without providing clues to their identity. In fact, we leak information about ourselves every time we speak or write. For instance, I can tell you're from the Midwest, am I right?"

"Yes, but what gave it away? Since I've been in broadcasting, I've tried to get rid of any farm accent," I answer.

"Just the way you still say your Rs," Alexander says with a grin. "But it is subtle. I can tell you've changed some of your other speech patterns. See, in forensic linguistics, we also analyze the choice of each word used, how words are combined, and it provides essential information about a suspect. The vocabulary, the grammar and in the case of a spoken communication, the pronunciation used can provide clues to the communicator's origin, age, gender, possible behavioral disorders and even factors such as the criminal sophistication, threat potential and authenticity of the speaker."

"And have you had a chance to review the 1985 ransom call in the Dwayne Meyers case and the letters his widow, Denise, received over the past number of years?"

Alexander pulls papers out from his notebook, and I recognize them as copies of Denise's notes. Even viewing it upside down, I can read the transcript of the call made by the kidnappers 28 years ago.

"The call was 12 seconds long. I'll read it in, roughly, the East Coast group dialect of the probable White male in his 30s: 'We got Meyehs. If you wanna see him alive, put one-point-five mil in the trashcan on the cohner of Grovah and Washington by midnight tomorrah. No cops or Meyehs is dead.'"

The agent makes eye contact with me. "We can tell by his changing Rs into Hs—such as Meyehs instead of Meyers, and cohner instead of corner—that he's probably originally from New York City, and more specifically the Bronx. However, everyone also has his or her own 'idiolect,' or speech habits peculiar to that particular person."

He shifts pages and spreads the various notes demanding money in a neat row. Using magazine and newspapers, the letters were cut out to say: "leave $5k under the matt. dont tell anywon," and "we need $5k or we kill yor kids."

"These notes were most likely produced by someone different," Alexander explains. "We believe this person purposely misspelled words like 'matt' and 'anywon' in an attempt to disguise their identity. Probably a lower-level criminal being groomed for bigger things. But we were able to determine the newspaper used was *The Arizona Republic,* and the magazine was *Gun Lover's Book of Weapons.* We believe this person was also a White male in his 40s when he started and 60s more recently, originally from the Midwest but now living in Arizona."

"Wow. So, were you able to positively identify the people who made the call and sent the notes?"

Special Agent Alexander cocks his head and produces a sly smile as he gathers his papers. "Now, that information has to come from Chandler PD. But let's just say we have corroborated their findings." He stacks up the papers and puts them back in the notebook. The pen goes into his inside pocket, and he stands and tucks the leather book under his arm.

"Just one more question…how are you able to deal with such bad guys day after day?" I ask, rising.

Alexander pauses, turning to stare through the window that looks out over Chandler's growing downtown area. "I attempt to create boundaries between my personal and my professional life. I have a family that is very supportive of what I do, and that helps a lot." He turns back to me. "We see a lot of pain and suffering, and the FBI monitors the long-term effects on us. Meanwhile, we rely on our faith, our families and friends and we try to do kind things for others. Most importantly, and what keeps me going, is to always focus on our mission to protect and defend the innocent."

The statement hangs in the air between the veteran FBI agent and me.

"Thank you very much, Special Agent Alexander," I say quietly, putting out my hand to his. He shakes it again.

"You're welcome, and best of luck to you."

With that, Geoffrey Alexander turns and walks crisply out the door.

Mysterious music fades up full and under, and I begin speaking.

"Welcome back to 'Murder in the Air Mystery Theatre.' I'm Lauren Price. We're nearing the thrilling conclusion of 'Frightful Fun House'—as we find out who is responsible for the two deaths at the Davidson Amusement Carnival.

"At the closed-down carnival, there are no rides swirling, no carousels spinning, no people laughing or screaming. Only the sound of hammering somewhere, as a carny works on a repair."

There's a sound effect of a loud banging on wood.

"The police detective who questioned the suspects earlier walks through the silenced carnival, accompanied by the private investigator and the young carnival couple. He flashes his badge as he enters the office trailer of Davidson Amusement."

"Police. I need to talk to one of your people," he says loudly.

I read: "A woman Liz saw earlier, wearing a white coat, and the male doctor rise from their desks."

"Yes, may we help you?" the woman asks.

"Yeah, where is Benjamin B. Brooks, your accountant? We need to ask him a few more questions," the detective says.

"Um, Ben didn't come in this...I mean, he just hasn't arrived yet this morning," the man stutters.

"Really? It's 11:30 already. Is he always this late?" the detective asks suspiciously.

"Oh, no, he's usually very—" The woman catches herself. "Uh, he is known for his promptness. Maybe he's sick today."

"Where would we find him?" the private investigator asks.

"Here, we'll show you," the man says.

He walks the detective, private investigator and Liz and Brad out the door, down behind the midway to a small trailer. The detective knocks on the door and waits. No answer. He knocks again. Again, no answer.

"Ya got a key for this trailer?" the detective asks. "Otherwise, we're gonna bust in. I got a search warrant for his living quarters."

There are sound effects of a piece of paper slapping into someone's hand, a jangling ring of keys, and the opening of a squeaky door.

The trailer is devoid of everything personal—no kitchen, bedroom or bathroom items. The detective opens a closet door. Empty.

"Looks like he skipped town," the PI says.

"We'll put out a BOLO for him," the detective says. "He can't get far."

Theme music from the mystery theatre fades in full and goes under my voice.

"What happened to the little man keeping the books? Or was he cooking the books? Will the police find him and bring him to justice? You won't want to miss the final chapter of 'Murder in the Air Mystery Theatre.' I'm Lauren Price. Goodnight."

CHAPTER 14

TUESDAY, APRIL 23

I speed dial Ron from my cell phone.

"The past 24 hours have been the longest in my life," I say breathlessly to Ron. "I'm sorry, I couldn't say a word."

"What's going on?"

"Turn on KWLF. Top of the hour news. Finally got the cold case solved."

"Good job. Call me later."

I turn up the newsroom speakers and hear "...with their 82 to 76 win over Michigan, Louisville is the new NC-double-A champion. I'm Dan Murray for KWLF sports. News is next."

The urgent sound of the hourly news music jingle leads off promptly at 5 p.m. The night-side anchor, Dennis, gives a thumbs-up to me through the glass announcer booth just before he starts to read his copy:

ANNOUNCER VOICEOVER:
Good evening. This is the KWLF five o'clock news. I'm Dennis Anaya. A stunning conclusion to a 28-year-old cold case that KWLF has been investigating...and recently helped Chandler police solve. What was thought to be just another tragic ending of a businessman's life during the savings-and-loan crisis of 1985...turns out to involve a former police officer using drugs and blackmail—all in the name of family. Here's Lisa Powers with the story:

LISA VOICEOVER:
This was indeed a cold case conundrum: seemingly no new leads, no updates, no way of figuring out why Chandler resident Dwayne Meyers—president of a small community bank—was found killed at close range in an abandoned warehouse at age 43. Meyers' bank was in trouble from over-lending to developers who had few assets. His young widow, now Denise Richardson, and mother of their two small children, was also in the process of filing for divorce, believing her husband was being reckless with their family's future.

A subsequent ransom demand was assumed to be part of an influence-peddling scheme gone bad, but after the kidnappers made off with more than one-point-five million dollars—despite being under surveillance by police—Meyers was found dead, and the leads dried up.

Denise received a five million dollar life insurance payout, and lived well for a few years. But that's when demands for yet more money started—a detail she chose to withhold from law enforcement until recently.

DENISE RICHARDSON SOUNDBITE:
"He...they threatened to kill my children."

LISA VOICEOVER:
Now, nearly wiped out by 20 years of payoffs to the unknown criminals, Denise also disclosed another pertinent detail: her late ex-husband used heroin, and the ransom notes received over the years had nothing to do with developers, but rather with drug dealers.

Chandler Police Detective Joe Johnstone helps piece together the puzzle.

JOHNSTONE SOUNDBITE:
"There were rumors at the time that someone from inside the department might have been involved, but nothing was ever confirmed until we analyzed the old evidence again. Ballistics tests on casings found near Meyers' body and during a shooting incident earlier this month at Ms. Richardson's home in Sedona were a match. In addition, a Texas crime scene investigator was able to conduct additional examinations of duct tape found on the victim's ankles—and discovered the fingerprints of former Chandler patrol officer William Jay, originally from New York, who had resigned shortly after Meyers' death, reportedly to care for his disabled brother."

LISA VOICEOVER:

Police found Jay visiting his sibling, Lennie, at a group home in Phoenix, where he admitted needing the money for his brother's increasingly expensive care. An FBI forensic linguistic expert was able to determine Jay's voice was the same as on the original ransom call back in 1985. Jay is now in Maricopa County Jail, where he has also named additional suspects in the original murder and subsequent demands for money.

Meanwhile, Denise, her adult children and her three grandchildren are safe and glad to be out from under further ransom demands.

DENISE SOUNDBITE:

"I want to thank police and Lisa for all their help to solve this case and catch the men who have tormented me for so many years."

LISA VOICEOVER:

Reporting for KWLF-FM, I'm Lisa Powers.

With two steaming cups of coffee on the table, Ron and I sit at the same 24-hour eatery where we had lunch last week with Bruce and Evelyn. Only today it is just the two of us.

"I still don't get how this Jay fella could fly under the radar for so many years," Ron says, sipping his drink.

"I think George Ware felt so guilty about his partner's death that the other cops just assumed he was involved and made life very tough for him. He started drinking heavily, managed to get a psychological disability pension, and police figured, case closed. It was all Jay could do to stay on the good side of the drug dealers and keep his brother cared for. Johnstone thinks the guy will probably get some kind of a plea deal, partly because of his age, since he's given up his accomplices and he's the only family his brother has."

There's silence as we sit in thought. I look at my aging friend and think *what an unlikely pair we are.*

"So, changing the subject, that 'date' last week with the four of us was quite the disaster, wouldn't you say?" I shake my head in disbelief, staring at my coffee. When Ron doesn't answer, I look up and see him with a remembering smile on his face. "Tell me we were at the same lunch?"

Ron adjusts his oxygen cannula and warms up his beverage from the coffee canister on the table.

"Actually, I thought it went pretty well," he looks down, as if a little embarrassed. "Evelyn's invited me for dinner at her place next week." His boldness returns. "Hey, how about you and TV Bruce? We had a deal, ya know."

"A deal? Hold on. I went out with him, you went out with her, we're even, end of deal. Besides, you were supposed to ask *her* out, not the other way around, so this next date doesn't count."

A beat. "Maybe not to you, but it does to me." Ron blushes under his two-day beard growth, and I smile.

"Well, Ron Thompson, you do like her after all," I chuckle. "I told you she was a nice lady."

The server drops off our check. "Let me know if you want anything else," he says without stopping.

I pull out my credit card and put it on top of the ticket. "And since I can't get anyone to take the kittens, I guess I'm going to keep them."

"Thought you said you didn't have time to take care of cats?" Ron says.

"Evelyn says she'll help. Cats are pretty independent, and having two, they can keep each other company. Plus, it is nice to come home to them."

"Well, I guess that's a start..." Ron smiles.

"Huh?" I don't get his meaning.

"Never mind. So, have you named them?"

"I think so. I went through the usual male and female companions: Lucy and Ricky, Elizabeth and Richard, Bogie and Bacall, but I've decided on Castle and Beckett after the characters in the TV cop show."

"Hmm. Fitting," Ron grunts.

The Murder Mystery podcast theme music fades in, and my voice begins.

"You're listening to a 'Murder in the Air Mystery Theatre' podcast. This is the last chapter in the latest episode, 'Frightful Fun House,' where an unassuming bookkeeper for the Davidson Amusement Carnival is suspected of killing two people in different towns—just to boost attendance. But now Benjamin B. Brooks is nowhere to be found—and police believe he fled to escape punishment."

A cacophony of sounds from a large carnival fills the air. Screams from people on midway rides pierce through the music of a carousel, engine noises and hawkers' taunts.

A door opens and a small bell jingles.

"May I help you, sir?" asks a woman with a Southern drawl.

"My name is Darryl Jones," says Benjamin B. Brooks' voice. "I'm here about the accountant position."

"Why, that's wonderful. Let me get our manager," she smiles, picking up the phone. "Harry, you have someone here who's applying for Joe's old job." She listens and hangs up. "He'll be right out."

An office door opens and Harry, a stocky man with thick arms and a very red face, walks out. He sticks out his hand to Ben/Darryl.

"How d'you do?" Harry bellows. "We could sure use your help with our books. C'mon inta my office, Mr....?"

"Jones. Darryl Jones," Ben says.

They sit down at chairs around a small desk piled with papers.

"So, where do ya come from, Mr. Jones?"

"Well, I most recently worked for a wonderful family carnival...but times were getting pretty tough," he says.

"Oh, don't I know it!" Harry says. "It's not easy, especially in this economy. You won't mind giving me some references so I can call 'em, do ya?"

"I'm afraid that won't be possible," Ben/Darryl lies. "They went out of business about a year ago. I took some time off, did some traveling and decided I missed life on the carnival circuit."

"Always hate to hear when another entertainment venue closes. So, tell me—can you help us be as profitable as possible, if ya know what I mean?"

"Oh, yes, I have a few tricks up my sleeve," Ben/Darryl says.

The mystery theatre theme music begins. My voice returns.

"So it looks like our accountant is trying to start all over again. Will he use his same old tricks and kill again? We may never know— unless the unsolved deaths land in some police officer's cold case file. I'm Lauren Price, your host. Other voices in this show were performed by Ron Thompson. Thanks for listening...and be careful: there might be 'Murder in the Air.' Good night."

The End

GLOSSARY

VO / voiceover – the voice of an off-screen narrator, announcer, or the like

SOT / sound on tape, or sound bite – a brief, striking remark or statement excerpted from an audiotape or videotape for insertion in a broadcast news story

NATSOT / natural sound on tape – audio recorded with sounds of the environment or surroundings

SFX / sound effects – any sound, other than music or speech, artificially reproduced to create an effect in a dramatic presentation, as the sound effect of a storm or a creaking door

UNDER – audio term referring to music heard under the voiceover

FULL – audio term referring to music heard at full sound

PACER – Public Access to Court Electronic Records

DMV – Department of Motor Vehicles

DB – dead body

GSW – gunshot wound

BOLO – be on the lookout, an advisory transmitted to law enforcement personnel to look for a specific vehicle, person, etc.

ABOUT THE AUTHOR

Laurie Fagen is a long-time "writer by habit" who has written for radio and television news; corporate video, films and documentaries; and magazines and newspapers.

An honorable mention in Alfred Hitchcock Mystery Magazine's Mysterious Photograph short story contest and a life-long love of reading whodunits led to three published short stories in Sisters in Crime Desert Sleuths Chapter anthologies.

Former publisher of a Chandler, AZ community newspaper with her late husband, Geoff Hancock, she is also a jazz singer and artist.

A member of Sisters in Crime (SinC), Fagen lives in Chandler with her two kitties, Jazz and Phantom.

.

Also by Laurie Fagen

Equalizer
Prequel to **Fade Out**

Coming face-to-face with danger herself, radio reporter Lisa Powers tracks down the murderer of a key witness in a money-laundering scheme.

The cold case of a Jane Doe near Lisa's age hits close to home, and her fancy footwork helps nail a Native American moccasin maker.

Lisa juggles her budding romance with an assistant DA while writing podcast stories about a too-real haunted house.

Made in the USA
San Bernardino, CA
13 April 2016